"So the reason you won't  **the only reason, is becau** **boss?" Molly held her br**

Zeke stared at her for a second, then glanced away. "No. Not the only reason. For another, you're a parent, and you know my take on having a family of my own, so getting involved would be wrong."

"I thought you said the right woman could turn you around, change your mind," she countered. She was going to lose in this back-and-forth.

"You're not the right woman, Molly. You can't be. Because you're my administrative assistant. End of story. Shall we go?" he added...tensely.

"In a second. I just want to understand. You kissed me last night because...?"

He let out a breath and looked down at the ground. "A little crush, I guess. I like you. Clearly, we have a great rapport and you're lovely, Molly."

She was swooning. *Lovely. Lovely. Lovely.*

"And for the reasons I stated," he added, "that kiss, our rapport, any of it, can't be explored further. But it's all right because I've already figured out a solution."

She almost puckered up.

Go ahead, kiss me passionately. If you're thinking that'll get me out of your system, you're so wrong, bucko.

DAWSON FAMILY RANCH:
Life, love, legacy in Wyoming

Dear Reader,

Thirty-one-year-old single mom of a baby girl Molly Orton has always accepted herself as a plain Jane. Conservative pantsuits, sensible shoes, very little makeup—that's good old Molly. But when she lands a job as administrative assistant to the man she's been secretly in love with since high school, Molly has a plan to get her sexy boss, Zeke Dawson, to notice her beyond her efficiency in the office.

Until something even bigger is standing in her way. Zeke is hoping to win the heart of Molly's gorgeous best friend—and he's counting on his admin's help. With Molly determined to be her own fairy godmother to make Zeke hers, there are lots of secrets and surprises in store for both Molly and Zeke and the folks of Bear Ridge, Wyoming...

I hope you enjoy Zeke and Molly's story. A special note: coming April 2021 will be Ford and Danica's story in *Wyoming Matchmaker*. Feel free to write me with any comments or questions at MelissaSenate@yahoo.com and visit my website, melissasenate.com, for more info about me and my books. For lots of photos of my cat and dog, friend me over on Facebook: Facebook.com/melissasenate.

Happy reading!

Melissa Senate

Wyoming
Cinderella

MELISSA SENATE

HARLEQUIN
SPECIAL
EDITION

HARLEQUIN®
SPECIAL EDITION™

Recycling programs
for this product may
not exist in your area.

ISBN-13: 978-1-335-40464-0

Wyoming Cinderella

Copyright © 2021 by Melissa Senate

This edition published by arrangement with Harlequin Books S.A.

For questions and comments about the quality of this book, please contact us at CustomerService@Harlequin.com.

Harlequin Enterprises ULC
22 Adelaide St. West, 40th Floor
Toronto, Ontario M5H 4E3, Canada
www.Harlequin.com

Printed in U.S.A.

Melissa Senate has written many novels for Harlequin and other publishers, including her debut, *See Jane Date*, which was made into a TV movie. She also wrote seven books for Harlequin Special Edition under the pen name Meg Maxwell. Her novels have been published in over twenty-five countries. Melissa lives on the coast of Maine with her teenage son; their rescue shepherd mix, Flash; and a lap cat named Cleo. For more information, please visit her website, melissasenate.com.

Books by Melissa Senate

Harlequin Special Edition

Dawson Family Ranch

For the Twins' Sake
Wyoming Special Delivery
A Family for a Week
The Long Awaited Christmas Wish

Furever Yours

A New Leash on Love

Montana Mavericks: What Happened to Beatrix?

The Cowboy's Comeback

Montana Mavericks: Six Brides for Six Brothers

Rust Creek Falls Cinderella

Montana Mavericks: The Lonelyhearts Ranch

The Maverick's Baby-in-Waiting

Visit the Author Profile page
at Harlequin.com for more titles.

In memory of my dear grandmother.

Chapter One

There she was.

Danica Dunbar. The woman of Zeke Dawson's dreams for as long as he could remember. She stood chatting with another woman in front of Bear Ridge Realty on Main Street. Zeke hadn't seen Danica since they'd graduated from high school thirteen years ago, when he'd left town and tried not to look back. He'd never forgotten her, though.

Back in middle school and high school, when he'd have a bad day—and those were plentiful—he'd see Danica walking down the halls, her long, wavy, light blond hair flowing behind her, and the fight he'd had with his dad would leave his head. He'd find his father passed out drunk on the front porch in the middle of winter, no coat, he and his siblings using all their strength to pull him inside, and then at school, he'd see Danica by her locker, dabbing on strawberry-scented lip balm, and it was like magic: his home life evaporated. She'd always had a boyfriend and the rare time she was single, Zeke was dating someone who'd already bought a dress for whatever school dance, so they'd never had a chance. He'd probably spoken to her only a handful of times back then.

Danica looked just the same, too, beautiful in her long red wool coat and shiny black heels. Zeke stood at the crosswalk, waiting for the light to change, surprised that he wasn't thunderstruck or hit by lightning, that he didn't hear a marching band with cymbals clanging in his head, something to signify seeing Danica, star of his fantasies for so long, after all these years.

Maybe he was too old for that nonsense. At thirty-one, Zeke was a workaholic who'd quit the rat race—just last week—and had opened his own consulting firm here in Bear Ridge. He'd spent months on that decision, but last Christmas, when he was visiting his siblings at the family ranch, he'd heard Danica was getting divorced, and that info had been added to the Pros side about moving back to Bear Ridge from Cheyenne. Not that he was glad she'd gone through such a terrible life upheaval and heartache. But they were both finally available at the same time—and Zeke was going to make his move.

Danica headed into the realty office. Interesting. Was she a Realtor? He was in the market for a house. A perfect reason to reacquaint. The woman she'd been chatting with stopped in front of his own office—Dawson Solutions, Inc.—a few doors down and appeared to be giving herself a once-over in the glass windowpane.

Ah. That had to be Molly Orton, his two o'clock. She was ten minutes early—a good sign in his book. He'd been interviewing nonstop the past few days, and no one had been quite right for the position of his administrative assistant. He'd just spent the past hour complaining about that over burgers with two of his brothers at the diner.

The light finally turned green and he headed across Main Street, his interviewee frowning at her reflection as she tried to tuck a long brown spiral curl into the low bun at the nape of her neck. The bun exploded, wild dark curls springing everywhere. He smiled and held back a bit, giving her a chance to redo the bun. She nodded at herself, then headed inside, glanced around and sat down in one of his new leather club chairs in the reception area.

Zeke approached the office, the matte silver letters spelling out Dawson Solutions, Inc. giving him a deep sense of satisfaction. He'd never expected to move home and open his own business, but circumstances—from the call of family and his pint-size relatives to the breakup from hell with a colleague—had worn him down.

He pulled open the door, his interviewee popping to her feet with her hand extended. He shook it—warm and firm and smooth. Molly had taken off her long puffy coat and was wearing a light beige pantsuit with a scarf at her neck. A silver pin in the shape of a cat was on her lapel.

"I'm Molly Orton, here to interview for the administrative assistant position," she said, that long spiral curl zinging out of the bun again. She shoved it behind her ear, a dimple in her right cheek appearing as she added, "Oh, but I'm sure you know that. I mean, we went to high school together. Middle school. Elementary, too. We were in the same kindergarten class. Mrs. Piedmont with those sparkly red cat's-eye glasses. Gosh, I loved her."

They'd gone to school together? Her name hadn't

registered at all when he'd gone over her application and résumé.

"I don't remember Mrs. Piedmont or her glasses," he said, taking off his coat and hanging it beside hers on the wrought-iron coatrack. "Though the name sounds kind of familiar. I've been gone from Bear Ridge a long time." Over the years, Zeke would be surprised by a random memory flitting into his head, some good, some bad. He'd always tried to limit his thoughts on his hometown to his talisman, Danica Dunbar. "Glad to be back, though," he added with a smile. That was true.

Molly started to say something but then clamped her lips shut, her brown eyes widening a bit as she glanced out the front window. He turned to see what had snagged her attention. Nothing out of the ordinary. A few people were crossing Main Street, including the barber from the next block walking his elderly dachshund, and an older woman wheeling a baby stroller with a white box balancing on the handles.

"So, let's head to my office. Coffee?" he asked, gesturing toward a short hall. "My sister gave me a great macadamia-nut blend as an office-warming. I could go for a cup myself." He led the way, appreciating the space he'd overhauled last week: the gray walls, the abstract-art carpet tiles, the sleek charcoal metal and leather furnishings, and the paintings and illustrations. He stopped in front of the coffee station set up on a credenza.

Molly Orton was staring out the front window again. Hmm. Did she have an attention issue? Would she be staring out the window instead of compiling lists of companies that he needed for research? Staring out instead of answering the phone?

She snapped her attention back to him. "I'd love a cup. And your sister is Daisy Dawson, right? I don't know her, really, but Bear Ridge is a small town and of course everyone knows the Dawson Family Guest Ranch. You're one of six siblings." Her gaze moved to the window again.

He set the coffee maker to brew, disappointed that he'd likely have to keep interviewing. He'd been so impressed with Molly's résumé. Solid experience. Not a single typo. But she couldn't even make small talk without getting distracted?

She was right about the ranch; everyone did know it—once upon a time because of how his father had destroyed the original place and now for what a beloved, popular fixture the rebuilt guest ranch had become in under a year. He nodded and reached for two silver Dawson Solutions mugs. "They've all moved back home, too, and four of them are married with children. My oldest brother, Ford—he's a cop here in town—and I are the lone holdouts, but—"

The earsplitting wail of a baby interrupted him.

Molly frowned and looked toward the window again. He did, too. The baby in the stroller—maybe a year old—was screaming bloody murder. As the woman pushing the stroller approached the sidewalk, leaning back the handles to raise the wheels over the curb, the box that had been resting on the handles fell off into the street.

"WAAAAAH!" came another bloodcurdling wail.

Molly slapped a palm to her forehead. "Excuse me for just one moment," she said, and went racing out the door. He was right behind her. She hurried to the baby, undoing the straps and lifting the little girl out, holding her against the jacket of her pantsuit. "It's okay, sweetsums, Mommy's got you." She patted the little back, the baby letting out a big yawn.

Ah. Suddenly things made sense.

"Mom, are you okay?" Molly asked the older woman, who looked like she was on the verge of tears.

"I'm okay," her mother said. "But I doubt the

cake is." She pointed at the white box in the street by the curb.

Zeke tried to pick up the box, but as he did, the box fell apart and something resembling a cake— lots of pink and white—slid out and landed on his very expensive Italian leather shoes.

"Oh, dear," Molly's mother said.

Molly grimaced, shifting the baby in her arms. "I'm so sorry about your shoes. I'll pay for a new pair, of course."

"Out of her first paycheck, maybe?" her mother asked with a sly smile.

Zeke grinned at her mother. He liked her. He liked both of them.

"Hey, no worries," he said, flicking his right foot to get a wedge of cake with lots of pink frosting off his shoe. "I'm sorrier the cake got wrecked. Strawberry shortcake? My favorite, too."

The two women looked at each other, and he could see relief flitting over their expressions. Zeke could easily see the family resemblance. The mother also had the wild curls, though her hair stopped at her chin, and they both had big brown eyes. "Don't kill me, honey," Molly's mother said. "I shouldn't have brought Lucy anywhere near your interview, but I guess she saw you through the window and wanted her mama." She turned to Zeke and thrust out her hand. "Have I even introduced myself? Abby Orton, Molly's mom. And that little darling is Lucy. She's a year old today. Isn't she just precious?" She walked over to Molly and made a funny face at her grandbaby, reaching out her arms.

"Lucy, you go with Nana, okay, sweetie-kins? Mommy will you see in a little while at home for your party."

The baby started screaming again, holding out her arms for her mother.

Molly sighed. "Or I could just leave now since I completely bombed this job interview," she said under her breath. "I apologize for wasting your time, Mr. Dawson."

"Zeke. And of course you didn't bomb or waste anything. In fact, I'd say rushing out of anywhere for a family emergency is a sign that you know your priorities."

Molly's eyes widened.

Her mother beamed. "Oh, she does. Molly is the *best* mother. And she's on her own. I tell you, it's not easy being a single working mother of a year-old baby, but Molly makes it work. She's so organized and efficient!"

"Mom," Molly whispered, her cheeks flushed.

Lucy let out a giant yawn and this time went right into Nana's arms.

"I'll just get my grandbaby home," Abby said. "See you later, honey. Good luck!" she added before sliding a hopeful look at Zeke.

He watched her mother wheel a quiet Lucy down Main Street, turning at the corner. "Well, let me just get as much of the cake as I can onto the bottom of the box and into that trash can," he said, "and then we'll head back in."

"I'll help," she said.

They scooped the destroyed strawberry short-cake onto a section of the box and got it into the trash can on the corner. Above the sweet smell of the cake he inhaled the faint scent of something spicy, Molly's perfume.

"I'll completely understand if you want to call a halt to the interview," she said, tucking another escaped curl behind her ear, a small glob of frosting on the sleeve of her jacket.

"Are you kidding? With your very impressive résumé? Not a chance. And I meant what I said. If my kid was screeching outside while my mom was trying to deal with that and carry a birthday cake that just dropped, I'd go help, too. That you did wins you interview points."

Her brown eyes lit up. "So we can start over?"

"Tell you what. You go home and be with your birthday girl. I'll see you first thing Monday morning."

Molly tilted her head. "We'll resume the interview then?"

"The job is yours, Molly. Welcome to Dawson Solutions." He quickly ran down the excellent benefits package as they ferried cake on the battered box pieces to the trash can.

In the ten minutes he'd been in her company, he'd learned quite a bit about Molly Orton and he knew she was the candidate he was looking for. He didn't have to ask his list of questions. She'd worked for an accounting firm for the past three years, her boss a known jerk (per a quick vetting of her résumé), which told him she knew her way around difficult people and stuck it through—to a breaking point, since she'd quit that job a few days ago, all detailed in her cover letter. He liked the honestly. And based on how she'd handled herself just now, he knew she'd be able to take on trying scenarios, key in a consultancy where nervous clients called at all hours and expected their problems to be handled. Zeke Dawson was a handler. And he needed his admin to be one, too.

"Wow, that's even better than I hoped. Thank you, Zeke. I accept!"

He smiled. "I'll see you Monday at nine a.m., then. I'd like to take you out to lunch to welcome you to the office and I can fill you in on the particulars of the firm and all that."

"Great," she said. She hurried inside the office and put on her coat, then came back out. "Thanks again," she said, and then practically ran down the street and disappeared around the corner.

He had a good feeling about hiring Molly. There was something about her, something efficient and capable and calm. She'd be an asset with clients who came to the office for meetings.

As he was about to head back inside Dawson Solutions he realized he forgot to bring up Danica Dunbar; he probably could have very easily found out from Molly if Danica was seriously dating anyone. But for once, he'd forgotten all about his old dream girl. He'd ask Molly about Danica at lunch on Monday.

His to-do list was long, even for the weekend to get ready for the official opening of his business. But he could cross off a major one—he now had his administrative assistant.

And if things went his way, he was about to have the woman of his dreams.

* * *

Molly stopped around the corner and closed her eyes, her heart beating so fast she was surprised she didn't implode.

As if seeing Zeke Dawson again—and for a job interview—after all these years hadn't been enough, there was her crying daughter, quite possibly the loudest baby in Bear Ridge, and her mom and the cake landing right on Zeke's expensive shoes.

But she'd gotten the job! She could hardly believe she had. *Mission accomplished, Molly*, she cheered herself on as she resumed walking. The position was perfect for her, and as a bonus, she'd see Zeke Dawson—tall, gorgeous, sexy, dark-haired, Caribbean Sea–eyed—every weekday from nine to five. Who knew what could happen in a two-person office, working late at night, sharing takeout, an unexpected kiss leading to her finally feeling Zeke's lips on her, his hands on her. She grinned at the fantasy.

But then she came back to earth fast. She was a realist who had never let her daydreams get the better of her. Molly had been secretly in love with Zeke Dawson since middle school and he had never noticed her. Now he would never see her as anything other than his trusty administrative assistant.

There had been sixty-two kids in their graduating class at Bear Ridge High School. Everyone "knew" each other. Or *of* each other. But some people didn't stick in others' minds, and Molly had always been one of them. When Zeke had first walked into the office for their interview and she'd stood to shake his hand, her knees had wobbled. She'd been so consumed by seeing him up close and personal that she'd rambled on about their kindergarten teacher's glasses, for Pete's sake. She'd worried she might go mute when she came face-to-face with him, so at least she'd said something.

And she was no longer that quiet girl with zero confidence, the plain Jane sidekick to the school beauty who no one ever noticed. Molly might not have changed all that much physically since senior year—though she'd given up glasses for contacts because Lucy liked to grab them and shake them in her little fists—but she had in all other ways. Between the divorce and motherhood, Molly had come into her own. She knew who she was and she liked that person.

She *could* finally go for Zeke Dawson, make her move. Except there were two problems with that. One: now he was her boss. There was probably a policy against dating coworkers, particularly a subordinate, in the Dawson Solutions, Inc. company manual. And even if she "seized the day," as her mom was always telling her to do, and made her feelings known, Zeke was just too gorgeous and sexy for the plain Jane in the pantsuit and sensible pumps. He'd let her down easy and she'd still have to work with him. Appreciated for her mind if not her face and body. That would actually make continuing on as his admin bearable, now that she thought about it. She frowned—didn't she just say she wasn't that same old girl without any confidence?

Two: the fact that Molly's name and face hadn't registered with Zeke one bit did irk her. He hadn't remembered she existed. Out of sixty-two kids in their graduating class? Come on. She'd be invisible to him all over again, and the new Molly Orton would not let herself fall for someone that shallow. She owed herself and her daughter better than that. How could she guide Lucy in the ways of womanhood if she was mooning over a man who didn't even remember her? Molly *had* thought about dolling up for the interview; she actually did own a few push-up bras that she'd gotten for her bridal shower. But she'd learned fast that trying to be someone she wasn't was never the answer. Molly wasn't a push-up-bra type. She wore the teensiest bit of makeup—a dab of powder, a little mascara, a bit of rosy blush—as part of her professional look. She was understated—except when it came to her hair, which just couldn't be controlled. She was who she was, and Zeke was who he was: out of her league on a looks level.

But he'd never been a town golden boy. Far from it. Growing up, everyone had heard the stories about his dad, a flirtatious drunk. His father had been married three or four times and was a notorious womanizer. She remembered hearing about classmates' dads chasing him down Main Street for making a pass at their wives. After running his parents' fifty-year-old popular guest ranch into the ground, Bo Dawson had died just over a year ago, from alcoholism complications. Life as one of his six kids couldn't have been easy. Zeke had been through some hard stuff from an early age.

And Molly hadn't been in love with him half her life just because he was so good-looking. Back in school he had a reputation for being a nice guy who'd always stood up for the underdog. Given how he'd reacted just now, he was still the same wonderful guy.

Who had *never* noticed her. Not even when he'd walk down the halls of Bear Ridge High, unable to take his eyes off her best friend, Danica, and Molly had been right beside her—for years! Granted, every guy had mooned over Danica in school, walking into open lockers and doors and water fountains. Molly had been invisible.

And now? She'd hardly be invisible in her new role. Molly would just wait and see what happened. They were both single and that meant something *could* develop between them. If he wasn't attracted to her, fine. She'd move on from thinking of him as a remote possibility. Somehow.

She started walking home but suddenly froze. Someone *else* was single again. For the first time since high school: Danica Dunbar. Molly's bestie, newly divorced and *looking*, was five-nine, model thin with big boobs, long blond hair, angelic blue eyes, a warm, funny personality and had the opposite sex drooling everywhere she went. Her best friend would surely notice Zeke. He was the hottest guy in town.

Then again, despite being one of the kindest people Molly knew, Danica had a thing for men who didn't deserve her. She liked bad boys, always had. Whether slick in a suit or brooding in a leather jacket on a motorcycle. Molly had had lunch today with Danica, just before the interview, Danica asking for advice about getting back out there in the dating world. Bless her sweet heart for thinking Molly could possibly offer tips on men to a Christie Brinkley lookalike. Molly had told Danica to try changing her type—nice guys only. No bad boys. Molly wanted her friend to take her good advice—as long as she didn't go for Zeke Dawson, a nice guy who *looked* like a bad boy in the smoldering sense.

Hmm, she thought as she turned onto Oak Lane. Maybe Molly would have to break her vow never to tell *anyone* how she felt about Zeke. One thing Molly had never shared with Danica was her crush on him—not back in middle school or high school, when she'd hoped so hard he'd mysteriously ask her to the prom (he hadn't), and not now, when he'd suddenly come back to town after a thirteen-year-absence. In high school, another girlfriend of theirs had had an insane crush on a major pop star that had consumed her, and Molly had always felt being secretly in love with Zeke was kind of like that. Unattainable. Ridiculous. Pointless. Molly—smart and sensible—had faced facts even in elementary school when not one boy asked her to the fifth-grade semiformal. If Danica knew how Molly felt about Zeke, her sweet, loyal friend would never look twice at him. Molly had no doubt of that. But she'd feel silly even bringing it up. *Um, Danica,*

I'm in love with Zeke Dawson and may or may not go for him and he'll never go for me, but if he asks you out, can you say no?

Maybe he'll ask you *out*, she reminded herself.

Molly pushed all that away and channeled a scene from one of her favorite movies, *Bridget Jones's Diary*, imagining Colin Firth telling Renée Zellweger he liked her, very much, just as she was.

She'd keep her secret to herself. And play it by the ole ear. After all, now that she'd be working with Zeke, he'd truly get to know her. And didn't her mom always say that to know Molly was to love her?

She grinned and kept walking. All she knew for sure was that Monday would be very interesting.

Chapter Two

Shifting the bakery box to his other hand, Zeke rang the doorbell at 102 Oak Lane, a small yellow cottage, the postage-stamp yard covered in snow from the last storm. After Molly left this afternoon, he'd gone into his office to do some prep for a few meetings he'd scheduled for Monday, but he'd been unable to stop thinking about the cake in the street. A baby's *birthday* cake. He had to replace it. There was only one bakery in town, and just down Main Street on the other side, so he'd gone there.

The door opened and there was Molly in yoga

pants and a Wyoming Cowboys sweatshirt, her gorgeous wild curls loose past her shoulders. She held a bunch of helium balloons—and frowned at the sight of him. "Zeke? You're not here to take it all back, are you? I *don't* have the job?"

He smiled. "You absolutely do. I just figured I'd bring you this." He held up the cake box. "A new and improved strawberry shortcake. I had them write *Happy 1st Birthday, Lucy* on it in pink."

She gasped, her free hand going to her chest, and stared at the box for a moment. "How incredibly thoughtful of you, Zeke. Wow. Thank you."

"Well, like I said, strawberry shortcake is my favorite, so I couldn't imagine Lucy not trying her very first slice. I mean, it *is* her birthday."

Molly grinned. "She's—"

"Waaah!" came a high-pitched shriek. "Waaah!"

"Uh-oh," Molly said. "I'd just got her down for her nap, too. Her party starts in two hours and I've got a ton to do. Usually my mom comes to my rescue but my cousin's son had to be picked up sick from school and my dad is superbusy with his new retirement venture, so I'm on my own."

The phone rang. Then another one rang. "Oh, God, landline and cell at the same time! Ahhh!" She threw her hands up in the air, the balloons drifting up to the ceiling. She slapped her hand to her forehead.

Zeke held back his smile. "Tell you what. You answer the phones and do what you need to. I'll go get Lucy. My brother Noah calls me the baby whisperer. I pick up one of his crying twins and they instantly stop bawling, little hands pulling my ears."

Her eyes brightened. "First door down that hallway!" she tossed over her shoulder as she ran for the phone on the coffee table. The landline was still blaring away.

"Waaah! Waaah!"

"Coming, Lucy," he called. He glanced around as he headed down the hall. The house was small but cozy, nicely decorated in what his sister would call beach-cottage-chic with white walls, pale blue sofas, pillows with embroidered starfish, shag rugs and lots of driftwood furnishing. He arrived at the nursery, *Lucy* stenciled on the door in pink and purple script. He went inside to find the baby girl screaming bloody murder again in her crib. She stood, holding on to the railing. "Hey, there," he said. "I've got you." The sound of his voice had her quiet for a moment, her big brown eyes, just like her mom's, fixed on him. She held up her arms.

He took off his suit jacket and tossed it on the

glider chair beside the window, then reached for the baby and brought her to his chest. "How does such a little human make such a big sound? Huh? Can you tell me that?"

Lucy didn't answer or even look up at him. She was too busy fighting her drooping eyes, her little fist grabbing at a button on his shirt. He patted and rubbed her back and sang her what he remembered of the "Itsy Bitsy Spider" song, and the baby's mouth gave a quirk, then the eyes finally closed for good.

"Success," he whispered with one final gentle pat. "How I'm the baby whisperer of Bear Ridge when I don't even want a baby of my own is beyond me, but some things are mysteries, right, Lucy?"

"Well, that's a shame. You really are the baby whisperer."

Startled, he turned to find Molly in the doorway, the balloons in her hand again.

"Usually when Lucy wakes up during a nap," she said, "especially early on, she's impossible to get back to sleep. I owe you—again."

He grinned. "Just the uncle touch. My brother Rex's baby girl is around Lucy's age and loves me. I'm her new favorite. Drives Rex nuts. He was the old favorite till I showed up in town."

Molly grinned. "Yup, Lucy's new favorite is my cousin Stella. She has a red heart tattooed above her eyebrow—for real, and wears sparkly green eyeshadow. No one can compete with all that fun glam."

He glanced down at the baby asleep in his arms. She really was precious, as her nana had called her. Big rosy cheeks, bow lips, curly brown hair that promised to be just like her mom's. She wore purple fleece pj's that said Baby Power across the front.

"I'll put her back in the crib," he said, heading over. He set her down, expecting her to screech any second, but she transferred perfectly, not a peep. His twin niece and nephew, Annabel and Chance, were champion nappers, but Tony, his sister Daisy's baby, required tricks.

In the two weeks he'd been back in town, he'd spent time with his siblings and had done some babysitting, making up for all the moments he'd missed. Being the uncle was easy; after an hour or two of playtime, he could leave. How his siblings had taken to parenthood was beyond him. They'd had the same cruddy upbringing he had. Noah and Daisy, his youngest siblings, had lost their mother when they were kids; they'd been raised by Bo Dawson. And they were the first two to marry and become parents. Not necessarily in that order, but still. They seemed like such naturals at it—the doting, the caretaking, the love. Everything. Axel and Rex, who he'd also thought the two least likely people alive to become dads, were now hoisting their own little ones and nieces and nephews up in the air, proudly wearing their Wyoming's Best Dad sweatshirts that Daisy had given them as stocking stuffers last Christmas. Was it the Bear Ridge water? Something in the air, maybe? The ranch soil? Now that he was back, would he suddenly turn into a family man? He didn't see it. He'd have to ask his brother Ford—the other holdout. As the eldest Dawson sibling, Ford had seen it all.

"How many nieces and nephews do you have?" Molly asked as they left the nursery and headed down the hall.

"Well, there are the twins—my brother Noah's kids. And Tony, my sister Daisy's son. Then there's Axel's son, Danny, who's two and will be getting a sibling soon. And Rex has Chloe. She'll be one soon. I think." He shot her a sheepish smile. "I might have all that completely wrong. My calendar tracks their birthdays."

She grinned. "Well, as your new admin, I can take over that."

"No way," he said. "I don't assign personal stuff. That's not your job."

Her entire face brightened and he was suddenly struck with the urge to kiss her.

Whoa. What? This was his new employee. In an oversize Wyoming Cowboys sweatshirt and navy yoga pants. Where had the burst of attraction come from? Molly wasn't his type at all. Danica Dunbar had always been his ideal and he'd been drawn to that look in college and at work over the years—tall busty blondes with easy laughter and long nails. He loved long, polished nails and jewelry that clinked.

Jada, his ex, was all of that, and she'd burned and betrayed him. So maybe the urge to kiss Molly—not tall, not blonde, not particularly busty, no makeup, short, unpolished nails and no jewelry, in sweats—was about a break in that type. His brain protecting him from what had happened in Cheyenne.

Except Danica was exactly that type. Then again, she was the original.

He glanced at Molly, suddenly confused by his crazy train of thoughts.

"Not to speak ill of my last boss," she said as she led the way into the kitchen, where she set the bakery box on the counter. "But ugh, what a jerk!

He had me send flowers to women he dated and even asked me to pick out sexy lingerie for his last girlfriend. I finally had had enough and quit without having another job lined up. Irresponsible, I know, given that I have a baby to support. But the last straw was when—" She clamped her mouth shut and turned away. "*Anyhoo.* Can I get you something to drink? Coffee?"

He frowned, wondering what she'd been about to say. He hated the idea of anyone harassing her or causing her grief. "Well, I can assure you that I run my office in a very professional manner."

But he had just been thinking about kissing her. She did have a lovely face, so warm and open, her lips plump and pink, the big brown eyes so intelligent and curious.

She laughed, loud and happy, the sound making him smile. He just *liked* Molly, liked being around her, liked her as a person. She was easy to talk to, easy to be with, and as his new employee, of course he was interested in her as a human being. She'd soon play a major role in his life. Of course he hadn't wanted to *kiss* her—he just enjoyed her company, was all.

"I don't have macadamia," she said, gesturing at her coffee maker, "but I do have hazelnut. And Jamaican Me Crazy. My personal favorite."

He'd actually love to sit down at her small, round kitchen table with the stained-glass vase of orange flowers and have a cup of her favorite coffee. Molly Orton relaxed him, and between opening his own consulting firm and moving back to his hometown, he'd been wound tight. But he couldn't stay. Unfortunately.

"Actually, I can't," he said. "I'm on babysitting duty for Axel's toddler. That kid keeps me on my toes. He's actually a faster runner than I am. Tell Lucy I said happy birthday, okay?"

She tilted her head, her wild curls falling to the side. "I sure will. And thank you again. For the cake. For being a baby whisperer." A phone rang again. "Never stops," she said. "I'm letting that go to voice mail. I have a *huge* extended family. And everyone wants to know what to get Lucy for her birthday. I keep telling my relatives and friends to just bring themselves, but I have a feeling this tiny house is going to be full of giant stuffed animals and Fisher-Price toys that make lots of noise."

He smiled. "Yup, you should see my siblings' houses. Except Ford's."

"Ah, yes, you said you two were the last hold-outs for marriage and kids."

"Well, he actually *wants* to get married, so it

won't be long before I'm the sole lone Dawson around the table at the next family event."

Unless of course things worked out with Danica Dunbar. If anyone could get him down the aisle and thinking about kids, she could. Life had a funny way of working out. Nothing would surprise Zeke Dawson anymore.

"You're not planning on getting married?" she asked. "Like *ever*?"

The phone rang again, interrupting a conversation he really didn't want to have, anyway, though he was the one who'd brought up the subject— twice, he realized. "I'll let you get that," he said. "Enjoy the party."

She gave him a warm nod and walked him to the door. "See you Monday. And thanks again, Zeke. Really."

The moment he was on the other side of the door of her little yellow cottage, he wanted to be back inside, talking, having that Jamaican Me Crazy coffee. When was the last time he talked so easily with a woman? Even with Jada, who he'd actually gotten serious about, their chemistry had been off but he'd ignored it because she was beautiful and they had so much in common. Until he discovered she was two-timing him with a rival and probably sharing company secrets that they'd talked about late at night in bed.

He'd even tossed marriage around in his head a few times before that, wondering if he could do it, be that man with all his bad memories of what marriage was. His dad had been married three times, widowed the last go-around, which had done a number on him. His mom, who lived on a small farm in Florida, had remarried and was happy, but whenever Zeke seriously thought about marriage and kids for himself, he'd feel his shirt collar tighten and a strange acidic sensation in his gut. Yeah, maybe he would talk to Ford, who had said a few times in the past couple months that he was ready to settle down. Zeke had no idea what that would even feel like—the *want*.

He glanced at Molly's door, at the winter wreath in the shape of a heart. Maybe it was time to get past all those old thoughts humming just below the surface. He might be a success at business, but his track record in romance had him in the red when it came to his personal life. If he was going to start dating Danica, he should be serious about it, expect the relationship to go somewhere. Her beautiful face came to mind again, but then Molly's face popped into his head and baby Lucy with a big slice of strawberry shortcake on her high chair.

He smiled, thinking of her enjoying the cake he'd brought over. He'd have to ask his brothers and sister if babies could even eat birthday cake. He really had no idea.

"See you Monday," he whispered to the door, vaguely aware that he was really looking forward to that.

On Sunday night, Molly laid out two possible first-day-of-work outfits on her bed, wishing she had more style. Navy or winter white. Bo-ring. Molly had always been a conservative dresser, neutrals—she was very fond of shades of beige—high necklines, small earrings. But now that she wanted a shot with Zeke Dawson, a man who not only brought over a new birthday cake for her baby girl—with writing on it—but had cared for her when she'd woken up from her nap so that Molly could answer her never-stop-ringing phone, she wanted to stand out just a little.

Enough to make Zeke see her as more than his capable new assistant.

"What do you think, sweetsums?" she asked Lucy, who was careening around Molly's bedroom in her ExerSaucer. Lucy wasn't quite walking yet.

"La pa!" Lucy said with a big grin, batting at the dancing monkey toy on the ExerSaucer.

The monkey wore a white T-shirt and yellow shorts. Molly glanced at the winter-white pantsuit with the sheer yellow scarf beside the navy pantsuit with the red floral scarf. Winter white and yellow scarf, it was.

She smiled and scooped out Lucy, giving her a snuggle. "You might not be talking yet, but you were a big help to me." Molly gave her a kiss on the cheek. "Let's get you to bed, and then I'll try on the outfit and accessorize." For that, she'd Face-Time the very stylish Danica.

As she got Lucy ready for bed and then settled the baby on her lap for a good-night story, she had that sensation again, one she'd had only a few times in her life. That something momentous, thrilling, full of possibilities was about to happen. She'd felt that way the night before her wedding to her now ex-husband, so hopeful about the future. And she'd felt that way all during her pregnancy, despite being unexpectedly single and scared. And she'd felt that way this past Friday afternoon when Zeke had hired her without an interview.

Molly glanced down at Lucy sprawled against her on the glider and realized she'd been so immersed in her thoughts she'd bored her baby girl to sleep. She'd just transferred Lucy to her crib when her iPad chimed. Danica on FaceTime.

"Just wishing you luck for the big first day to-morrow!" Danica said, her favorite green-cucumber mask covering her face. Amazing that even with a green face, Danica Dunbar—Grace Kelly regal meets Marilyn Monroe accessible—was as beau-tiful as ever. "Not that you need luck," she contin-ued. "You've got this!"

Ever since they'd met in second grade, opposites—even then—somehow becoming best friends, Dan-ica had rivaled Molly's parents, aunts and uncles, and eight first cousins as her biggest champion, and the Orton clan was hard to top.

At Lucy's birthday party, Molly had told Dan-ica all about the morning, and Danica had been stunned by Zeke's generosity. She'd wriggled her eyebrows and said, "Maybe the two of you will fall madly in love."

Molly had almost choked on the delicious piece of strawberry shortcake she'd been eating. But in-stead of saying: *God, I hope so*, she'd said, *Oh, no way. He's my boss. Gotta keep it professional. And I'm sure that's a rule of his, too. Or it should be.*

Why she'd said all that, she had no idea. Was she trying to actually invite Danica to go for him? She knew why she was afraid to put it out there that she was crazy about Zeke Dawson, but still.

"So which do you think, the winter white or

navy?" Molly asked, turning the camera to the two pantsuits on the bed.

"With your gorgeous dark hair, the white will really pop," Danica said. "Though I'm thinking the blue and red floral scarf instead of the yellow—I like the gravitas of that one with the white. Ooh, you should wear your lucky pearl-drop earrings and the watch your parents gave you for your twenty-first birthday."

Everyone needed a Danica. "What would I do without you?" Molly asked, turning the camera back to herself.

"What would *I* do without you?" Danica said, gingerly touching her green face to test if the mask was dry. "Because guess what, Mols. I'm taking your advice. From now on, I will *only* date nice guys."

Newly divorced, Danica had refused to date until that decree had landed in her mailbox, signed and official. She was now raring to go. Because Molly had had some dating experience—all from Converse County Singles, a local dating app—Danica actually sought out her help on getting back out there. Ha. Danica might have had her heart broken by her cheating ex, but she already had men asking her out left and right in the supermarket and drugstore and coffee shop. The last guy who even responded to Molly's profile had written: My ex-wife spent a fortune on hair straightening treatments. You'd never know she used to look like she stuck her finger in an electric socket. You should try that. Molly had typed back: You should try some manners, bucko. Then logged off permanently. Like she needed that?

"I've been thinking a lot about what you said at lunch on Friday," Danica continued. "About the red flags to watch out for on a first date. I've got them memorized."

Molly smiled. Yup, Danica had always been drawn to the Rhett Butlers, the James Deans, the Jordan Catalanos: the rebel with or without a cause. She liked tall, very good-looking men who made her work for their hearts. Ugh. Danica had been doing it since middle school. And all her boyfriends—and her husband—had one thing in common: they were not what Molly or her nana would call *nice*.

"If he drones on and on about himself and doesn't ask me a single question about myself, he's out," Danica said. "If he stares at the waitress's breasts or is rude to her while she's setting down our drinks, he's out. If he says anything that makes me cringe, he's out." She gave a nod. "Not one of my major or not so major relationships was nice. That's awful. Why didn't I see that before?"

"Eh, don't be so hard on yourself. We're thirty-one now. Divorced. Lived a little. A lot, actually. We're older and wiser and not about to make the same old mistakes. We know what we want!"

"I love you to death, Molly Orton. I really *don't* know what I'd do without you. And that's been true for almost twenty-five years. Call me after lunch with your boss tomorrow to tell me how the morning went. And I'll call you tomorrow tonight after my date with the bronc champ."

Rodeo stars could be nice, right? Molly would give him the benefit of the doubt because Danica was excited about the date. "One not-nice move, no nightcap, no coffee, no invitation in."

Danica's eyes widened. "Uh-oh. I can't even smile with this mask on. Better go wash it off. Have a great first day tomorrow!"

After Molly put away her iPad she tried on the winter-white pantsuit—and it did look good with the little sheer floral scarf and the jewelry Danica had recommended. Though, really, she shouldn't be trying this hard.

Or maybe she should be. When you really wanted something, you had to go for it. She finally had a chance—remote as it was—with Zeke Dawson in their two-person office, and she was taking it. She'd get a sense of their dynamic at work and go from there. Maybe they'd have no chemistry. Maybe she wouldn't develop any romantic feelings as she got to know him.

Right. Who was she trying to kid?

"Do babies eat cake?" Zeke asked his sister, Daisy, as she plopped her seven-month-old son, Tony, on his lap.

After a big Sunday family dinner, which he'd learned was a new family tradition for the Dawsons of the Dawson Family Guest Ranch, just he and Daisy sat in the living room of the farmhouse the siblings had grown up in. After his parents' divorce, Zeke, Rex and Axel, the children from Bo Dawson's second marriage, had spent half the time at their mother's house in town, but this place had always been "home." Zeke had been staying with Daisy, enjoying the extra time with Tony, who was one cute little guy, and access to all his nieces and nephews. Tony was content to sit and chew and shake his teething toy in the shape of a dinosaur.

"Well, they *can*," Daisy said, taking a sip of her coffee. "For special occasions. Like Tony's first birthday—he can definitely have a tiny piece of his own cake. But generally, babies shouldn't have sugar." She raised an eyebrow. "Why did you want to know?"

He told her about hiring his new administrative assistant. The entire story poured out of him, which was unusual. Zeke always held back; it was the way in business, and it had carried over into his personal life. He wasn't a schmoozer. Now he was telling his sister how he'd bought a replacement cake and brought it over to Molly's and had ended up singing the "Itsy Bitsy Spider" to the birthday girl.

He didn't mention the strange urge to kiss Molly—the opposite of his usual type. The opposite of Danica Dunbar, his dream woman since eighth grade.

Daisy was beaming. Which meant he'd said way too much. His sister was slightly obsessed with seeing all her brothers married and starting families. Her favorite pastime used to be trying to get them to move back home, and one by one, they all had. Noah was first—he'd actually taken on the role of rebuilding and renovating the ranch, and lived in the foreman's cabin—forewoman's he should say, since his wife, Sara, had that role, with their twin one-year-olds. Daisy, who'd come home pregnant and alone to help Noah with the grand reopening last summer, was now guest relations manager for the ranch, and she and her husband, Harrison, a businessman, lived in the farmhouse with Tony. Axel had built himself a log mansion on the far edge of the property that he shared with his expecting wife, Sadie, and their toddler, Danny. Rex had also built a house on the ranch, nestled back by the woods and mountains, for himself and his wife, Maisey, and their baby, Chloe. Ford was staying in the staff cabin that Rex's wife, the ranch nanny, had lived in before they'd become a couple.

Amazing. All six Dawsons actually living on the ranch. The past couple weeks, Zeke would run into one of his siblings while riding or helping out on the property, and they'd all marvel at the fact that they were back. Especially Ford, who'd once said buffalos would fly across Wyoming before he'd live in Bear Ridge again. Now he was a detective for the Bear Ridge Police Department as was Rex, a former U.S. Marshal. And here was Zeke, who'd figured Cheyenne was home, thinking about his options for a house. In town or on the ranch's vast property?

Daisy's blue eyes were twinkling, a sign she was playing matchmaker. "Office romance in the works? Babies have a way of bringing couples together. Look at Rex. He found a message in a bottle—a fifteen-year-old letter to Santa—brought it to the writer, who happened to be a single mom of a six-month-old, and bingo: he and Maisey are married now and raising baby Chloe together."

He ruffled Tony's wispy brown hair as the baby chewed on his teether. "Not gonna happen. First of all, I'm not planning on getting married. Or having kids. I've told you that. I have a ton of nieces and nephews to spoil. Second of all, I'm Molly's boss. There's no way I'd date her." There. Even if at some point he had a *second* urge to kiss her, he'd just remind himself that it was inappropriate. He should really create a human resources handbook on policies—including the dating of colleagues. As someone who'd gotten involved with a turned-out-to-be-shady coworker, he'd never do that again.

Again, Molly's face floated into his mind, all that lush, wild curly hair, the pretty brown eyes. He fought a smile at the thought of her in her sweats. She hadn't even started at Dawson Solutions yet, and he'd already seen her at home on a weekend. He'd soothed her baby back to sleep. They were clearly becoming friends, and they'd have a *friendly* working relationship—nothing wrong with that.

"Hmm, just you and her in the office, day after day, both working toward the shared goal of the success of Dawson Solutions, Inc.?" She grinned. "We'll see."

The thought of him and Molly working together was like a soothing balm. There was just something trustworthy and capable about her. He'd always considered himself a good judge of character, even if that had been blown to bits by Jada, a snake in a sexy pencil skirt and high heels, and he had a feeling he'd found an admin he could really count on.

He'd hardly ruin that by getting involved with her. And besides, there was only one woman in town he wanted—Danica Dunbar. "Trust me. It's not like that. I'm interested in someone else."

His sister practically bounced out of her chair— Daisy was a born matchmaker. "Ooh! Who? Someone I know?"

"I know her from school actually. She always had a boyfriend, though, and now she's single. Danica Dunbar."

Daisy rolled her eyes with a smile. "I should have known. The hot blonde Realtor, right?"

"She's not *just* a hot blonde, Daisy."

His sister tilted her head. "Oh? What else is she?"

"Well, I don't know her. Yet. But I'm sure she's as lovely a person inside as outside."

Daisy sipped her coffee. "Why assume that?"

Didn't he know better than to discuss his love life with his sister? "Maybe I should stay with Rex or Axel," he said, narrowing his eyes at her. Though she wasn't wrong. Given what happened with Jada and how she'd burned him, he couldn't assume anything. His trust level was at an all-time low. But he supposed when it came to Danica, there was something kind of mythical about her. He shook his head. He had to remember that Danica was a real person, not some fantasy.

Daisy laughed. "Just saying, Zeke."

"Anyway, I remember Danica from school. We had a few classes together over the years. She's perfectly nice. I think Molly was in some of those classes, too."

"You don't know?"

"I can't seem to remember her from school," he said. "Maybe she changed. Thirteen years is a long time."

"I'll check the yearbook," Daisy said, popping up.

"Why would you have my yearbook?" he asked.

"I'm the keeper of family treasures, heirlooms and memories. I have all your yearbooks." She went to the bookshelves flanking the stone fireplace and looked through the spines. "Yup, here it is." She pulled it out and sat back down, taking a sip of her coffee, then opening up. "What was her last name again?"

"Orton. Molly Orton."

Daisy flipped through pages. "Ah, here she is. She looks kinda familiar. I've probably seen her around town." She put the yearbook faceup on the couch beside him, then scooped up Tony from his lap. "I've gotta get him down for his nap. Back in ten."

"Have a good nap, champ," he said to Tony, standing to give the adorable, yawning tot a kiss on his head.

As Daisy headed upstairs, he sat back down and took a sip of his own coffee and looked at Molly's photo. Huh. He *did* remember her. She wore round silver eyeglasses and her mane of curly brown hair was pulled back into a ponytail. He would often see her and Danica walking the halls together or chatting in a class they all had. Her senior quote beside her photo was by Eleanor Roosevelt. *A woman is like a tea bag. You never know how strong she is until she gets in hot water.* Had Molly gotten into hot water? Then? Since? He stared at her picture, suddenly wanting to know more about her. But, of course, that would happen naturally staring tomorrow morning.

He flipped back a few pages until he got to the *D*s. Ah, there she was: Danica Dunbar. Damn, she was angelic looking. She'd barely changed in thirteen years. Her senior quote was by another famous Roosevelt—Theodore: *Believe you can and you're halfway there.*

He grinned. *I do believe.* They'd finally have their chance.

He'd definitely talk to Molly about Danica, try to get a little intel. He wouldn't be unprofessional about it; he wouldn't even mention his romantic interest. Maybe he'd ask Molly if she knew any great Realtors in town, and she'd mention Danica and offer a personal tidbit or three or ten. His plan was to stop in the realty and ask to meet with Danica about checking out houses in town. Who knew? They could go from a house to dinner and even to bed, depending how things went. He wouldn't be surprised if they had a whirlwind romance.

Daisy came back downstairs. "So, Zeke, about not planning to get married or have kids. You do know that Danica is your age, right? She probably wants to start a family."

He put the yearbook away. "Maybe I can be turned around by the right woman." Maybe. He really wasn't sure of that at all.

"Hmm, I'm liking the idea of you and Danica

together more and more," she said with a grin. "I need a new niece or nephew."

He laughed. "There are already a ton of tiny Dawsons."

"There can never be too many."

He glanced up at an artful black-and-white photo of Daisy, Harrison and little Tony in the main barn, the goats behind them. He tried to imagine himself in that photo with a wife, a baby. But he couldn't. Watching his family explode, the stories of his father's first marriage, his parents' divorce, his father's anguish at losing his third wife to cancer, which had exacerbated his drinking. Everything that made Zeke leave Bear Ridge at eighteen and put himself through night school while working in corporate mail rooms during the day, watching how the bigwigs walked and talked and dressed and acted until he himself became one—all those memories were still deep inside him. He didn't think about them much but he felt the blockage in his chest any time someone brought up marriage—and girlfriends had in the past. *Not for me, not a family man, I don't want kids...*

Could the woman of his dreams since middle school change all that? Maybe.

Believe you can and you're halfway there...

He just wasn't so sure he did believe it.

Chapter Three

At Molly's previous job, personal items were discouraged from "cluttering desks" and limited to a single three-by-five framed photograph in a steel-gray frame to match the cubicle walls. Here at Dawson Solutions, Inc., her desk was her domain, per her new boss. When she'd arrived this morning, Zeke had welcomed her with an African violet plant in a pretty pot, told her to get herself acclimated and to meet him in his office in thirty. Oh, and he'd gotten her favorite coffee and had made a pot, so help herself. *Swoon.*

With her Dawson Solutions, Inc. silver mug of

delicious coffee, she'd taken herself on a tour of
the office, opening cabinets, pawing through the
manuals for the high-tech printer at the side of her
desk, getting a feel for her new home away from
home. Then she'd knocked on Zeke's door, but
he'd been on the phone, the corporate lingo mixed
with down-home Western making her smile. Finally, she'd sat across from him, typing notes on
the iPad he'd furnished her with (she also had a
desktop and a thirteen-inch-laptop provided by the
office) as he'd gone over the business and protocol
and his vision for Dawson Solutions. She'd forced
herself to focus on what he was saying instead of
losing herself to his face, the melodic sound of
his deep voice. Companies, big and small, hired
Dawson Solutions to turn them around, either get
them out of the red or simply help grow. This was
essentially his job at the company he'd worked for
in Cheyenne, and he'd developed a reputation of
being the noncursing Gordon Ramsay of the business world.

She'd spent the morning listening to him take
calls with potential clients so that she understood
how he operated and what his clients sounded like,
and then he'd left for a meeting, leaving her to di-
gest all that. She'd gone back to her desk, spun
around on her high-tech ergonomic chair, almost

unable to believe this was her life now. A new job at an interesting company with the man of her dreams as a boss. A boss who made the coffee, no less.

And then, at lunchtime, he escorted her to Grill 307, a popular, upscale bar and grill about a quarter mile from the office. As he pulled out her chair, she almost felt like she was on a date with Zeke. He ordered the steak frites and she went for the swordfish tacos, and they talked about Bear Ridge and people they knew in common.

"So it turns out I do remember you from school," he said, poking at his salad. "I'm staying with my sister until I figure out what I want to do house-wise, and I mentioned to her that I hired someone from my graduating class, so she got out the yearbook."

He'd looked her up in the yearbook? Interesting. "Oh, God, that photo. Me in my Harry Potter phase—the round glasses."

He laughed. "We have a goat at the ranch named Hermione. And two chickens named Dumble and Dore."

She still couldn't get over that she, Molly Orton, was capable of making Zeke laugh. How many times had she imagined herself chatting with him by their lockers or running into him around town, her saying something so clever that he laughed and then looked longingly into her eyes, telling her that he'd never noticed how pretty she was before and what was wrong with him? She'd had many daydreams along those lines.

But she doubted he was thinking she was pretty right now. Personable, maybe.

You should wear more makeup, one of her Converse County Singles dates had the gall to say to her over coffee.

I'm fine as I am, she'd said, wishing she'd had a better comeback. Half of her always wanted to be polite and the other half longed to tell him to go jump in a lake.

You'd probably have more luck if you did a little something with yourself, he'd gone on as if he were a prize.

Look, bucko, you're the one who approached me on the app.

Converse County Singles: confidence buster. Though, granted, she did have a couple dates with men who were quite nice and polite and listened attentively and one of them had asked her on a second date. But then *she'd* been the rejecter, which had made her stomach hurt because she knew what getting rejected felt like: crud. But she hadn't been attracted to the guy on any level. Why was dating so hard?

Molly glanced at the women dotted around the restaurant. Most did seem glamorous, especially compared to her. Danica never left her house without adding beachy waves to her straight blond hair and she had an hour-long skin-care and makeup routine. But she'd been like that in sixth grade, loving CoverGirl as much as she loved working on their science experiments. In school, Molly had asked her most glamorous cousin, two years older and more a Danica than a Molly, how she could get girlier, and her cousin had responded that Molly was who she was and shouldn't fight her natural self. Her natural self didn't seem to interest the guys, though.

Zeke was about to pop a cherry tomato in his sexy mouth when his gaze shot to the door, and he sat up a bit straighter. Molly glanced over. Uh-oh. Danica had come in with two of her colleagues from the realty. Zeke's blue eyes were lit up like Christmas. Fooey.

"Molly, hi!" came Danica's voice as she passed by their table on the way to hers.

Her bestie was in her gorgeous long red wool coat and she wore her usual high heels, her blond hair in a chic low ponytail over her shoulder.

"Hi, hon," Molly said, her heart plummeting.

"You remember Zeke Dawson from high school, right? Zeke, Danica Dunbar."

As if she needed introduction.

Danica's gaze slid to Zeke and she smiled and extended her hand. "Sure I do. Captain of the baseball team, am I right? I think we had a couple classes together. History, I'm pretty sure."

"And Environmental Science," Zeke added, shaking her hand. "Nice to see you again."

Well, there it was. They'd formally been reintroduced and now they'd skip off into the sunset together, and Molly wouldn't even have a plus one for their wedding.

Two men sitting at the table beside theirs got up to leave, both in their thirties, attractive, in suits. One of them said to Danica, "You probably remember me from high school, too, but I was a couple grades ahead. Captain of the hockey team and I ran cross-country. I'm now a doctor in private practice. Orthopedics."

Molly glanced at Zeke, whose eyes were now narrowed on the interloper. So were Molly's. *Hello? Remember me? Yoo-hoo? We were paired up as partners on a special project for Spanish 4? I exist. I'm not invisible.*

But the doctor only had eyes for Danica. "I'd love to take you out to dinner—Saturday night?"

he continued. "Arabella's?" he added, naming the one very expensive and superromantic restaurant in Prairie City, the bigger, more bustling town a half hour away.

"I'd love to," Danica said, "but, to be very honest, I'm just getting back out there in the dating world and have dates scheduled practically every night the next two weeks. Thank you, though."

Both the interloper *and* Zeke deflated, their strong shoulders lowering, their disappointment palpable.

The doctor handed her his card. "Well, keep this. When you're free, I'd love to hear from you. You're absolutely gorgeous."

The two men left and Danica sighed. "Just once I'd like a guy to ask me out by saying, 'We have so much in common, let's go to x, y, z since we both love that.' Ugh—I hate the focus on how I look."

Molly loved Danica, but where was her tiny violin, seriously?

Then again, she knew what Danica meant. Her friend had been judged on her looks since she was a child, the apple of everyone's eye because of her big blue eyes and sweet, stunning face and beautiful blond hair. Molly was invisible for being average and Danica had a spotlight because she was gorgeous. She could see where *both* would have their downsides.

Danica's coworkers were waving her over to their table. "Ooh, better get going. Nice to see you again, Zeke. And talk to you tonight, Mols."

The waiter was hovering with their entrees, and as he set down the plates, Molly felt herself relax, her appetite back and then some. Danica's dance card was full—there'd be no room for anyone for at least two weeks, and maybe she'd find her Mr. Right among them. Maybe Zeke was safe. Correction: Molly was safe. For the next two weeks, anyway.

"Believe that guy?" Zeke asked with an awkward smile as he stabbed a fry with his fork. "A little slick."

Oh, great. He was jealous.

"She gets that a lot," Molly said, taking a bite of a swordfish taco.

"So you two are close friends?" he asked, swiping the fry in spicy garlic dip.

"Besties since second grade."

He stared at her for a moment as if debating something, then leaned in close. "I'll be honest. I've had a crush on Danica since eighth grade. And I totally get what she's saying about her looks being the focus. A match is about chemistry, shared interests, values. Not the superficial. I mean, maybe attraction alone will suffice for a couple dates, but not a relationship."

Hmm. Interesting. "So you *do* want a relationship?" she asked. "You did say you're not interested in marriage or kids."

He cleared his throat as if either giving himself time to come up with an answer or because she'd struck a bit of a nerve. "I think it's possible that the right woman could change my mind."

"I'm glad to hear that. That you're open." She felt her cheeks flush. "I mean, I'm divorced and should be all bitter but I feel hopeful about love and romance and maybe getting remarried one day, despite not exactly having success with Converse County Singles. Men want the Danicas of the world."

He stared at her again and now she wished she could take it all back. Why on earth had she said any of that? She made herself sound like the chopped liver she was.

"I think what anyone wants is the right person," he said, cutting a piece of his steak. "Maybe Danica is and maybe she isn't, but I have to get to know her to determine that, right? And since she's booked solid for two weeks, that's not going to happen unless I make it happen."

Molly swallowed. "How would you do that?"

"By asking you for pointers?" he said. "If you're comfortable with that, I mean. She just said she wants a guy to ask her out because of common ground. So maybe it would help if I knew a little about her, her hobbies, that kind of thing. I'm sure something she's interested in will match with something I'm interested in, and I can start from there. And if she has any pet peeves, I can avoid making them. You know, those little things that drive you nuts."

"Well, we definitely all have those," she said, her heart plummeting. She could forget about Zeke noticing her when his heart was completely taken with Danica.

She took another bite of her excellent swordfish taco, her appetite diminishing by the second.

"Name three of yours," he said, surprising her. She'd been getting used to their lunch conversation being the Danica Hour, but now it had come back to her.

"Just three?" she quipped. "I have tons."

But the biggest? When the man I'm secretly in love with is secretly in love with someone else.

"Like when people talk to the TV," she added. "Ugh. I hate that. How am I supposed to hear the show?"

He laughed. "I talk to the TV! Like 'Come on, you clearly blind ump—he was safe! Gimme a break!'"

She grinned. "Yeah, like that. Or during scary movies when the person you're watching with says, 'Don't go in there! No, don't it.' Good grief. Can I watch in peace?"

He chuckled and drank his iced tea. "What else?"

She put down her fork. "When people hum or sing while I'm talking to them. Hello? Are you listening? People who drive the speed limit in the fast lane. Close talkers. Memes that I don't understand. Interrupters. Grammar police. Being a jerk and then saying, 'I was just kidding, jeez.' People who start sentence with, 'No offense, but…' You do mean offense! Oh, and people who forget my name—hi, Milly, Mara, Moira."

Zeke was laughing hard, which puffed her up a little. She might not be the woman of his dreams but she could make him laugh. Except you know who else had a great sense of humor? Danica. "I have just one pet peeve," he said.

Molly leaned forward, dying to know.

"When my siblings bring up embarrassing stories about me," he said. "'Hey, Zeke, remember when you cried like a baby when Fluffers the chicken died? Hey, Zeke, remember how you got lost on the ranch and the police found you in a tree?'"

"Isn't that what siblings are for? Ragging on you? Keeping you humble? Though I am an only child. But I have my cousins to rag me."

He nodded. "I can definitely always count on my siblings. No matter what. That's really what got me back to Bear Ridge."

"What do you mean?" she asked, taking the last bite of her taco.

He glanced up at her, as if he hadn't realized he'd said that aloud. "Well, a relationship went deep south in Cheyenne. It was the final straw. I'd feel like hell and go walking around the city to try to shake it off, to get filled up somehow, and nothing worked. But every time I'd come visit the ranch, see my family, hold one of my little relatives, I'd feel connected. I finally realized that I not only wanted my family around me, that I needed them."

Aww. "I definitely know what you mean. When I was going through my divorce, my parents and nana and aunts and uncles and cousins all rallied around me. I was never alone. Three a.m., I could call my mom sobbing my eyes out and she'd not only not hang up on me, she'd come over with Ben & Jerry's."

He smiled. "Family is everything."

Yeah, family is everything. So why wouldn't you want to build one of your own. A wife. Children. That's what it's all about.

He cleared his throat, which she was beginning to see was his way of seguing from "how did we get on his too-personal level" to a lighter note. He began telling her about Hermione, the runaway goat at the ranch, and how there would be many Dawsons climbing Clover Mountain looking for the escape artist.

She liked the funny stories. But she wanted to get down and dirty personal. Share everything. Talk about everything. She loved that they could and had—before he'd remembered that she was actually his admin and adopted a more professional manner, even sitting back more.

The waiter came over to clear their plates and take dessert orders.

"I say we split something decadent for your first day," he said. "You pick."

As if she needed more evidence that he was her kind of guy. "Mocha-fudge cheesecake, for sure," she said. "Like chocolate cake or apple pie could touch that."

"Agree. You're my kind of gal, Molly Orton."

She almost gasped. She'd been thinking the exact same thing.

See, she wanted to say. We *are the ones who have everything in common.* She'd spent a few summer vacations at his family's guest ranch back when his grandparents ran it, and Danica wasn't a fan of "roughing it." Her friend liked hotels with all the amenities—so did Molly—but Danica didn't love the smell of horses or the sound of roosters at four thirty in the morning. Plus, from their chitchat on the way to the restaurant, Molly had learned she had the following in common with Zeke: they both loved Mexican and Indian food, old movies, hikes on breezy days, swimming in oceans, lakes, ponds and pools, the Wyoming Cowboys—their local minor league baseball team—seventies rock and family get-togethers.

Family is everything...

Every minute in Zeke's company, she fell just a little bit harder for him.

"So give me one piece of advice in wooing Danica," he said, taking out his wallet to pay the bill.

Humph. She'd been hoping their easy conversation and common interests would have him focused more on her, but Molly was once again the

Amazing Invisible Woman. Good for advice and taking care of business. Otherwise: didn't exist.

"Oh," she said in her best professional tone as she glanced at her watch. "Zeke, if you're going to make it to Prairie City by three for your meeting, you should really be on the road in no later than fifteen minutes."

He glanced at his own watch. "I knew hiring you was the best thing I'd ever done. My mind was definitely elsewhere."

Yeah, on Danica.

As they headed back to the office, she was struck with a brainstorm.

She didn't see Zeke and Danica together, and not because she saw herself and Zeke together. She couldn't quite put her finger on why, but knowing Danica so well, and having gotten to know Zeke a bit—nope. They might have attraction but there wouldn't be any *chemistry*. And Molly and Zeke— they definitely had it.

So Molly could be helpful without actually leading her dream man to another woman. He'd quickly see they weren't right for each other, and maybe spending some outside-of-the-office time with Molly to discuss his love life would make him see her in a hot new light. It *could* happen.

"Zeke, I have an idea. You've got a packed afternoon. Why don't you swing by my house tonight and I can give you some tips?"

His gorgeous face brightened. "Sounds great. Seven thirty?"

"Perfect."

Well, it wasn't, but it was a start. And Molly was taking it.

"No turning back now," Zeke said to his brother Ford as they stood on the front lawn of Ford's new house in their down jackets, Stetsons and gloves, the February bite sharper now that the sun had set.

Ford had texted Zeke earlier that he'd signed on the dotted line and was now an official Bear Ridge, Wyoming, resident. Since Zeke wanted to pick his brother's brain about a couple things, especially after the unexpected encounter with Danica while having lunch with Molly this afternoon, he'd suggested a quick celebration dinner at a good Italian restaurant to toast the new digs and Zeke's new firm. But they'd had so much to talk about and there'd been so many interruptions at the restaurant, people coming up to say hello—Ford had already become a local hero for cracking a missing person's case involving a runaway teenager and bringing him home safe—that Zeke hadn't had a chance to get too personal.

He could see why his brother had chosen this house. Very close to the police station in the center of town, yet tucked with just a handful of homes at the far end of a dead end street that led to walking trails, Ford's new home was a classic white farmhouse. He was planning to adopt two dogs once he was more settled and wanted to be near woods. Ford had taken him on the tour of the inside, and it somehow managed to be updated with all the high-tech latest and true to its turn-of-the-last-century beginnings.

"Nope," Ford said, looking up at the house. "No turning back. This is it, home sweet home." He glanced at the big oak in the yard. "I can see a tire swing here. Tree house in the back."

Amazing. Zeke would never get used to the new and completely different Ford Dawson. At thirty-six, Ford was the oldest of the six siblings. He'd been through it all, seen it all—both as a child of Bo Dawson and as a city cop in Cheyenne until just a couple months ago.

Zeke slung an arm around his brother's shoulder. "As I recall, you once said buffalo would fly before you moved back to Bear Ridge. Now look at you. Homeowner. Thinking about tree houses. And there's only one reason why someone would build a tree house. For kids."

Ford jabbed his thumb backward at himself. "Hey, I'm no spring chicken. I'm thirty-six. People change, grow, get past stuff. I'm thinking six kids. Big family, like we had."

Speaking of... "Let me ask you something. How'd you get from the Ford I knew to Ford 2.0 who actually wants to get married and have children? When and how did it happen?"

Ford looked at Zeke, a smile forming. "Interesting question. Sounds like someone is thinking about settling down himself. Who's the lady?"

Sometimes he forgot Ford was a detective. Zeke had always looked up to Ford, sought his advice. Growing up, his eldest brother had always been his go-to when he was pissed off about their dad. Ford wasn't just the oldest; he also didn't share a mother with any of them so Zeke would often take off for wherever Ford was, whether at his dad's or his mom's if he needed some space from his brothers Axel and Rex, and Ford always seemed to get it. "Listen, Detective, this is about you, not me."

"Nah, it's about you."

Zeke half scowled. "Fine, it's about me. There's a woman I've had a crazy crush on since middle school and she's now single. She's my age so it's reasonable to assume she'll be interested in marriage and kids. Well, Daisy pointed that out."

Ford nodded. "Whoa. You talked to Daisy about this? The matchmaker of the Dawson Family Guest Ranch? You must be far gone for this woman."

"I am. And in fact, in about a half hour, I'm due at my new assistant's house for pointers on how to make Danica mine. Turns out Molly and Danica are best friends."

Ford looked at him like he'd grown another head. "Um, you know you're not *still* in high school, right?"

Zeke shrugged. "Hey, I can use all the help I can get. Danica looks like a supermodel. And she seems really nice."

"Seems? Oh, so you don't actually *know* this woman you've been in love with half your life?"

Zeke narrowed his eyes at his brother. "Who are you…Daisy? You know how it is."

"Nope. I once did. Not anymore. A gorgeous face alone doesn't do anything for me anymore."

"Really? Why not?" Zeke asked.

"Time, experience, maturity. Who the hell knows. Don't get me wrong—I appreciate a beautiful woman. But I'm looking for a lot more. A life partner. Sickness and health, and all that."

It was exactly that *life partner* aspect that got Zeke all tied up in knots. He just couldn't see himself coming home to someone other than a great

German shepherd or golden retriever, perhaps. Between his upbringing and his last disaster of a relationship, marriage just wasn't on his radar. "It's not like I'm being shallow by pursuing Danica. She could be incredibly kind and giving and funny."

"*Could be* are the key words, Zeke."

"Well, if her best friend is Molly, then Danica has to be great. Because Molly is."

Ford eyed him. "What's Molly like?"

Her wild dark curls, big brown eyes and sweet face floated into his mind. "Smart, really funny, easy to talk to. I got really lucky that she applied for the position."

"Now *those* are the traits you want to go for, Zeke."

"I know," he said, rolling his eyes. "And I'm sure Danica is all that, too. But even if Molly *were* my type, she's my administrative assistant. That means she's off-limits, anyway."

"Oh, so we're back to your type? Supermodels?"

Zeke thought about Jada, also tall, 32-D, pencil skirts, tiny pastel-colored jackets and high heels. Her perfume had driven him nuts, some erotic, spicy scent. Had she been particularly funny or easy to talk to? No. She was smart, though. But yes, if he really thought about the two of them at dinner or in bed and walking around Prairie City's farmer's market, they'd had little in common and less chemistry except sexually. She'd never gotten his jokes, wasn't interested in hiking—one of Zeke's favorite things to do—didn't eat any food with carbs, another of Zeke's favorites.

"What type is Molly?" Ford asked.

Ford really did have the right job. What was this, an interrogation? And Zeke was suspected of being a shallow cad?

"She's…" His administrative assistant came to mind again. Molly in her pantsuit. Molly in her Wyoming Cowboys sweatshirt and leggings. Molly holding her baby girl against her, patting her back. Her quick laugh, easy smile, the funny stories she'd told him during lunch about her big extended family. "Well, I don't like the idea of relegating someone to a type. That's not cool. But she's…nice, I guess."

"You mean 'friend-zoned' because she doesn't look like a model."

"No, I mean…" He didn't know what he meant. "I've been interested in Danica for a long time and want to pursue her. End of story. Jeez, back off."

Ford smiled and held up his hands. "I should tell you—I know for a fact that Danica Dunbar is plenty nice. She was my Realtor on this house."

"See?" Zeke said. "I was right." He nodded up at the property. "All the more reason for me to get to know her that way since I'm in the market for a house. And fine—I'll make sure there's something between us, chemistry, common ground. If Danica will even go out with me. She's booked up solid for the next two weeks. I heard her telling some buff doctor who asked her out."

Ford laughed. "Well, then, go get your pointers from Molly. Good luck. You're a good guy, Zeke. One of the best people I know. I'm sure Danica will see that. Plus, you look like me, so you've got that going for you, too."

Zeke grinned. All the Dawson brothers looked alike with their dark hair and blue eyes. Plus they were all six foot one or two, and favored black Stetsons. Often Zeke would be walking down Main Street and someone would call, "Hey, Axel" or "How's it going, Noah?" He'd lift up his hat, and the person would say, "Oh, sorry, I thought you were…" The Dawson clan all took after Dad, including Daisy, who had lighter hair but the blue eyes and the height and the features. None of them was surprised that Bo Dawson's genes were the dominant ones over their mothers'.

Ford tipped his hat. "Just sharing some of my hard-earned wisdom, lil bro."

Zeke appreciated that Ford always gave it to him straight, didn't say what Zeke wanted to hear but what he *needed* to hear.

"But you want to know how I know I'm ready for marriage and kids when I'd spent so long running from making commitments?" Ford asked.

Zeke nodded. "Yeah, exactly that. How do you know?"

"Well, I just felt a restlessness. I started feeling some kind of hum, thrum, whatever you want to call it, for something more, something different. It's just a feeling deep inside and right on the surface, too. All I know is it's what really brought me home, Zeke."

Zeke stared at the big oak, at the branch where a tire swing would likely go. He could picture a bunch of little Fords lying on their bellies and full of expectant glee, Ford giving the tire a big push. "Well, if a hum or thrum of that brought me home, I don't feel it, deep down or otherwise."

"So maybe the right woman *will* change that. You'll see. But, Zeke. One more thing you should know. Expect the unexpected."

"Don't I always? Hey, Ford," he added. "Why didn't you ask out Danica when she was showing you houses?"

"She's beautiful, no doubt, but I said black, she

said white. I said up, she said down. Honestly, I'm not sure how she managed to find me a house."

Zeke grinned. "Good. Less competition with you out of the running."

He pulled out his phone and glanced at the time: 7:22. He was expected at Molly's at seven thirty. Another person who would give it to him straight, judging from their conversations so far. The thought of her—his trusty assistant—had goose bumps breaking out along the nape of his neck. He couldn't get to her house fast enough. Within a half hour he'd have his intel, and who knew? Maybe Danica would soon be showing him a house for the two of *them*.

Yup, hiring Molly Orton was proving be a very smart move on all kinds of levels.

And really, Ford was great and all, but he was way off here. This thing with Danica wasn't about type. Zeke not thinking of Molly as anything other than his admin also had nothing to do with type. *I mean, come on.* He was crazily attracted to Danica and had been forever. So he didn't *know* her– know her yet. He would. And she'd be as lovely on the inside as she was on the outside. No doubt.

As he'd said, if she was Molly-approved as a best friend, Danica had to be wonderful.

Chapter Four

Once again, when Zeke arrived at Molly's, both of her phones were ringing—and the doorbell.

"You're very popular," he said as she held the door open wide and gestured for him to come in before racing toward the living room for her cell phone on the coffee table. She took the call in the hallway, so to give her some privacy he went into the living room.

Lucy was standing up in a playpen waving a rattling rabbit toy. She stared at him, her big brown eyes saying: *Pick me up, please!*

He smiled at her and scooped her out, the eyes on him.

"Ba," she said, waving the rabbit with a big smile, showing him her adorable baby teeth.

"You don't say. So how are you, Lucy? Did you enjoy your birthday party? Did you get to try some strawberry shortcake?" He and Molly had been so busy at work today in setting up the office and going over how Dawson Solutions would operate, and they'd had so much to talk about over lunch, that the subject of Lucy's party hadn't had a chance to come up.

He heard Molly dashing into the kitchen for the landline and saying hello. From the gist he was able to overhear, someone was asking how her first day at her new job had gone.

"She sure did," Molly said, coming back into the living room and tossing her phone on the love seat. She had what seemed a pleasantly surprised look on her face when she saw Lucy in his arms. "My mom told my nana what happened with the cake she'd picked up on Friday, so Nana rushed out to the bakery to get a new cake and she told my aunts, who told my cousins, and do you want to know how many birthday cakes Lucy ended up with at her party? Eight."

He laughed. "Seriously?"

"Want a piece of red velvet? Chocolate? Lemon chiffon? Carrot with the best frosting I've ever had? Plus I have four strawberry shortcakes, including yours. I'll have you know I served yours first. My whole family thinks you're a saint now."

Zeke grinned. "Better than the alternative. And yes, I'll have a slice of whatever you recommend."

"I'll make coffee, too." She headed to the kitchen and he followed her. "And I know all about the alternative. My ex-husband and his wife stopped by the party so that they could say happy birthday to Lucy on her actual birthday even though they had their own celebration planned for the following day. My family gives the two of them the evil eye no matter how nice they are—and they are perfectly nice. Well, nice-*ish*. I mean, he did leave me for her and—" The color practically drained from her face. "Oh, God, did I just say that? Ignore."

He leaned against the kitchen counter and shook his head. "I like how you say what's on your mind. And as for your family and the stink eye? Team Molly. I get it." As he boosted Lucy in his arms, she grabbed his ear. He met the big eyes, full of happy curiosity. "Can you say *Ow*, Lucy? *Owww*."

Molly laughed and opened the refrigerator. "Yup, my ears have gotten the Lucy tug." She tapped her baby's nose. "I can take her if…she's heavy."

"Did I mention I can bench-press two hundred

and five pounds? This little darling is no problem. And she smells like baby shampoo. I think that scent is hard-wired into our brains to remind us of something good in our families." Now he was the one to kind of freeze. What had made him say something so leading?

"Definitely," she said, pulling out a white box. "I love that smell. When Lucy was an infant and I'd be scared to death about being on my own with her, a divorced mom, I'd just breathe in that scent and hold her close and I'd feel better."

He gave Molly a commiserating nod and rubbed Lucy's back. "I'm sure those days weren't easy. Especially at first."

"Oh, they weren't. Even with my parents and nana and aunts and uncles and cousins rallying around me. And boy, did I work hard to have an amicable relationship with my ex. I really had to train myself when he and his affair—now wife— would show up to pick up Lucy."

Lucy gave his ear another little tug. "Train yourself how?"

Molly set the box on the counter, grabbed a knife and two plates and cut two slices of what looked like red velvet cake. "Early on the arrangement was that they'd have her a few hours a couple times a week. The doorbell would ring, and I'd chant in my head, 'Now, Molly, when you open the door, do not, I repeat, do not stare them down or look like you're going to throw up. Do not make veiled, passive-aggressive or straight-out nasty comments to either of them, though you may want to. Though you *do* want to. Just smile and make pleasant chitchat. For Lucy's sake and your sanity. You'll be co-parenting with this guy not just for eighteen years, but forever. Sanity has to come first. *Lucy* has to come first.'"

He nodded. "Oh, trust me, I get that, too. Well, not personally since I've never been married. But my father's first wife, my brother Ford's mother, who left my dad, and my mother, his second wife, would have it out every drop-off or whenever they ran into each other in town—and this went on for years. Shouting, cursing. Right on Main Street. Or in front of our house, in front of all of us. What's worse, I think my father thought it was cute when his first and second wives would hurl insults at each other. Meanwhile, all of us would be standing there, shaking." He glanced out the window, at the snow clinging to the evergreens, to rid his head of the image. "Yeah, marriage? Not for me."

"I'm sorry you had to deal with that," she said. "Your family and me aside, I can think of many great marriages. My parents', for one. They've been married for thirty-three years. My dad is the cook of the family, always has been, and he plays music while he makes dinner. My mom will come in sniffing the air appreciatively, and he'll pull her into a slow dance to some eighties new-wave song by one of his favorite bands."

"Even a Flock of Seagulls?" he asked on a grin.

"I think they may have been his *very* favorite." She laughed and Lucy let out a giggle, too. "I wonder what the music will be when Lucy starts walking around with earphones, blocking out my nagging."

He smiled. "Maybe new wave will be back. You know, I really am glad to hear your parents are happily married. That's really nice. For them and for you. And just good to know. That there really are solid marriages out there."

She set the plates on the table, then reached into the cabinet and took out two mugs. "There definitely are. There are quite a few in my extended family. My great-aunt and great-uncle, Daphne and Dave, make out. Not that I want to see that."

Zeke laughed. "I hear ya. My dad and his third wife were always lip-locked. She was Noah and Daisy's mother but she passed away from cancer when they were young. They were married until the very end and I know he loved her very much, but the roving eye, the flirting, never stopped." He sighed. "It was nice to always see them hugging, though. Leah forgave him way too much—she actually accepted him as he was. Which I think is nuts. She was such a generous, kind person. Why let herself be treated that way by a snake?"

Molly headed over to the coffee maker, making a fresh pot. "Hmm. I guess she overlooked what she needed to in order to be married to the man she loved. Everyone makes their own compromises, choices."

"I guess," he said, wishing he hadn't brought it up. A few times when he was a teenager, school would let out and he'd walk along Main Street with his friends and one would say, "Hey, Zeke, isn't that your dad with his tongue down that redhead's throat in front of Billy's Bar?" And it always was. Sometimes a blonde, sometimes a redhead, sometimes a brunette. "I thought he was married to wife number five or something," the friend would add. And Zeke would just shrug and seethe.

"My mom and dad are huggers," she said fast as if wanting to keep the conversation on happier terms. "Always hugging. Every time I see them in each other's arms, I feel so comforted, even now at age thirty-one. Is that crazy?"

"Nope. Not at all. Who doesn't like a hug? Now

that I think about it, I'm kind of getting a hug from a one-year-old baby." He smiled at Lucy, who was staring at him, looking so intently at his face. At his nose. He really liked this kid. And he liked the lighter conversation—definitely.

"You know," Molly said, "after my ex and his wife dropped off Lucy's cake at her party, I happened to catch them walking back to their car and saw the way Lila took his hand, the way they embraced in the car for longer than the usual hug. I know it's hard for him—seeing his baby girl only a couple days a week, having her every other weekend. Yeah, he blew up our family, but it's still rough on him. I really saw it in how they were hugging—needing that hug. That helps me be kind to them."

"It's great that you have an amicable relationship," Zeke said. "And that you're so empathetic."

Molly poured two mugs of coffee and set them on the table. "Well, thanks. I do try. Plus, I hate to say it but Lila is actually nice and she's very sweet to Lucy. She's four months pregnant so Lucy will have a sibling—and close to her age. That's a good thing."

Except she said it kind of wistfully.

"Must be hard—the back and forth of joint custody," he said.

"It is. But Andrew and I divorced before Lucy was even born, so I'm used to it. And it really is important to me that Lucy will have her dad and his new family as an equally big part of her life. Gosh," she said. "How did we get on all this?"

"We do seem to talk easily," he said. Again he was struck by how little he and his own ex had talked. Their conversations had always been stilted and they rarely got into their pasts or families.

"How about we move coffee and cake into the living room—you can put Lucy in her playpen and we'll talk."

He headed into the living room, Molly following with a tray that she set on the coffee table. Shifting Lucy in his arms, he walked over to the window. "Lucy, look, snow flurries. When it starts to snow that means something good is about to happen."

Molly smiled. "You just made that up."

"Nope. My gram did. Whenever it would start to snow she'd say that to teach us to always expect the best and not the worst."

She smiled. "That's very sweet. I knew your gram. She was so kind." She held up a finger to indicate she'd be back, then disappeared into the kitchen.

She'd known his grandmother? How was that possible?

In a few minutes Molly was back with two forks. "We definitely need these," she said.

He smiled and set Lucy back in the playpen. The baby put down her bunny and grabbed her board book with a llama on the front.

"Does Lucy like llamas?" he asked, upping his chin at Lucy's book before sitting on one end of the three-seater sofa. "We have two at the ranch petting zoo. Oh, wait—they might be alpacas."

She laughed and sat at the other end of the sofa. "She's crazy for all animals, just like me when I was young. My parents took us to your family's ranch for a long weekend every summer when I was a kid—that's how I knew your grandmother. It was our big family trip." She smiled. "I loved the petting zoo so much. And the horses and the cafeteria, which had make-your-own sundaes. I would explore the riverfront near our cabin for hours. During one trip, a boy who'd been a real jerk to me—throwing pebbles at me, calling me four-eyes—had gotten assigned my favorite pony for a trail ride, and your grandmother saw me all teary and apparently had witnessed the kid being the devil because she made up some story to get the pony back for me to ride and put the boy on barn chores instead."

He grinned. "Yup, sounds like Gram. Champion of the underdog. She and my grandfather were wonderful people. The current ranch is a lot different than the old one. Have you been to the new version?"

She took a bite of cake and shook her head. "Out of my league financially. But maybe when Lucy's a lot older, I can take her. She'd love to see the llamas or alpacas—whichever they are—in person."

"Well, if you want a weekend away in the country, I can sneak you in. My brother Ford was staying in a small cabin on the ranch but he just bought a house and I'll probably be moving into the cabin until I figure out if I want to build on the outskirts of the ranch or buy in town. You and Lucy could bunk with me. There's a guest bedroom."

She stared at him. "Really? That would be amazing."

He cut into the red velvet cake. "Absolutely. And my sister-in-law Maisey runs the ranch daycare center and has a baby almost Lucy's age. You could have some time to yourself while Lucy plays with little buddies in the Kid Zone."

"Wow, this is sounding like a real vacation." She grinned. "But given that I just started a new job…I sure would love to take you up on that for a day trip one of these weekends."

"Next Sunday is supposed to be forty-five degrees and sunny—we'd still have to bundle up but sounds like good weather for a day at the ranch, and we can have lunch in the café. They still do make-your-own sundaes. Pen that in," he added with a definitive nod.

Her eyes widened and she seemed so happy he had the urge to pull Molly into a hug. Hold her close. Feel her against him.

Whoa there, he thought. He shook that very inappropriate thought right out of his head and cleared his throat. "So you said you could give me some tips about winning Danica's heart."

There. Back to the reason for his visit in the first place. Danica floated into his mind, her beautiful face and blue eyes and glossy lips that had starred in his dreams for so many years. Danica Dunbar. Why his mind had gone to holding Molly in his arms was beyond him. Maybe all that talk about hugging. *Focus, Dawson*, he told himself.

Molly ate another bite of cake. Then sipped her coffee. "Right. Danica. For a minute there, I almost forgot about that."

"Me, too," he said, sipping his own coffee. He *had* forgotten. "We always seem to have so much to talk about. There's not enough hours in the day."

She smiled. "I know what you mean."

He recalled how that hotshot doc had asked out

Danica right in the aisle of a restaurant while she'd been talking to someone else. Guys must ask her out day and night. "So given that Danica has so many dates and may likely be sick to death of men very soon, what's my way in?"

"I have to give you the age-old advice, Zeke. To be yourself. That's your best way in. But I *can* tell you that Danica absolutely hates vulgar jokes, so don't make any in her presence."

Ah. Exactly the type of information he was after. Molly was truly invaluable as a friend. "I don't make vulgar jokes so we're good there."

"And she loves the color blue. It's her favorite. So if you wear a blue suit or tie the day you plan to ask her out, it can't hurt. But, of course, you've got the blue eyes, so you could wear neon yellow— especially since your eyes are so…" She clamped her lips together and reached for her cup of coffee.

"So what?" he asked, suddenly unable to take his eyes off her soft-looking pink lips.

"Blue," she said quietly.

Her voice shook him out of his strange fascination with her mouth all of a sudden.

He forked a piece of cake, his gaze lingering on the way her camel-colored sweater rose up to reveal a swath of creamy bare skin. Why was he so…aware of her? Probably because he was getting to know her better and really liked her. Molly was great. Absolutely great. So of course he was noticing everything about her, the way good friends did.

"Any other tips to share?" he asked. "For beating out all the competition with Danica—getting that first date."

She tucked a long curl behind her ear and it immediately sprang back. He smiled and reached forward, tucking it himself.

"There," he said, a catch in his voice at how he'd touched her. He should not be touching her. Putting her hair anywhere. "Sorry," he said, sitting up very straight. "I don't know why I did that."

"My hair is insane. Mind of its own. I appreciated your help actually, since that curl wasn't minding me. Look, it listened to the boss. Staying put." She gave her head a little shake to demonstrate his curl-tucking prowess.

He stared at her lips. Pink. Soft. So inviting.

"Ba ga!" came Lucy's happy shout, and never had he been so happy to be interrupted by a baby.

"I know, sweetsies," Molly said. "Almost time for stories and bed."

He glanced over at Lucy, thinking he should get going and let Molly put her daughter to bed. He was probably keeping the baby awake. But Molly was cutting into her cake, and Lucy was playing quietly with her rabbit, chewing the tips of its teething ears. If he could just get back on track, get Molly and her lips out of his head, he could leave in peace. But right now, he was feeling…on edge.

"So anything else?" he asked. "The tips for winning Danica's heart, I mean." *Just keep Danica Dunbar in your head and you won't be thinking about kissing Molly. Holding her.*

Molly stared at him for a moment before responding, and he wondered if she could read his mind. She couldn't, right? She was so good at her job—in just one day—and was so smart and efficient that he wouldn't be surprised if she had superhuman capabilities.

Now he was *losing* his mind.

"Well, she likes Prairie City's bustling downtown," Molly said. "The antiques shops and interesting restaurants. She'd prefer a day of strolling and shopping and finding a great place to eat over, say, a hike up a mountain."

He nodded. "Note to self, do not invite Danica on a hike at the Dawson Family Guest Ranch. Though there are some amazing trails and Clover Mountain right there."

"Well, count me right in next Sunday. I love hikes and taking proud selfies at the summit. I'll put Lucy in her carrier. All we'll be missing is a friendly dog."

He *had* invited her to the ranch. Hmm. Maybe that was a huge mistake, given that he was having wildly inappropriate thoughts about Molly. His administrative assistant. Granted, he hadn't yet created his company handbook and there was no official policies against dating in the office, but there should be. He was her boss and that made a relationship between them out of the question.

Not that he was even interested in Molly romantically—God, where was this crazy train of thought taking him? Wrongville, that's where.

There's nothing wrong with friendship. You and Molly know each other from school—it's not as if you'd just met.

Even if he hadn't remembered her until he saw her photo in the yearbook.

Of course she and Lucy could come to the ranch and enjoy a Sunday with him as tour guide. In fact, spending some time with Molly outside of work might actually help him shake off these… thoughts. He'd just focus on her as his admin—not as a woman. Could he ask her to wear a pantsuit and little flowery scarf to the ranch on Saturday? That would help.

Losing. His. Mind.

Clearly.

"We have two ranch dogs," he said, trying to follow the conversation. "My brothers Axel and Rex both have amazing dogs—Dude and River. We can invite them—the dogs, not my brothers."

"Perfect," she said.

He stood up fast. "Well. This was great, Molly. I can't thank you enough for all the great advice you gave me about Danica." He was about to pass Lucy's playpen when she stood up and held out her arms.

"Wow, she likes you," Molly said. "You really are the baby whisperer of Wyoming."

He liked that honor his sister had bestowed on him but now Lucy wasn't just his admin's baby girl who he was perfectly comfortable with. Lucy was the baby girl of a woman—a *single and available* woman—who had his mind going haywire. The baby's little arms were still up, the big brown eyes glued to his face. He forced himself to relax and scooped her up. Lucy immediately grabbed his ear with a giggle.

"That's some grip she's got," he said, wishing Lucy would grab on to his collar instead so it would loosen and he could breathe.

Molly grinned. "Tell me about it. It's why I

never wear my glasses anymore. She broke two pairs before I wised up and got contacts."

He patted Lucy's back and set her back down in the playpen. "Night, Lucy. Sweet dreams." *Who is this guy?* he thought, blowing Lucy a kiss. Molly really did have him all kerfuffled.

He *had* dated a single mother or two early on, before he realized that he didn't want to be a dad, and he'd always been so awkward around their kids. With Lucy, he was the way he was with his nieces and nephews. Because Molly was his friend and *not* a romantic interest, doting on adorable Lucy didn't come with any expectations or strings.

Until now. But, of course, he could zap all this from his head with a cold shower and a good night's sleep, during which he'd dream of Danica Dunbar.

Yes. Back to normal. Everything was going to be fine.

Molly walked him to the door, taking his hat from the peg while he put on his jacket. "See you tomorrow, Zeke."

He felt a swell somewhere deep inside him at the thought. A comforting swell, a happy swell. Wait a minute. Yes. That was it.

Molly was beginning to feel like a best friend. He'd never had a female best friend and, in such a short time, his new admin had become dear to him. That was all this was. He wasn't used to having such a close female friend so of course he'd misread his feelings. He wasn't interested in kissing Molly or holding her. He just *liked* her. A lot.

She was becoming a real trusted buddy, a confidante, someone he could talk to about anything and everything. No wonder he was so happy about the idea of seeing her in the morning.

But as she handed him his hat and their fingers brushed, he found himself noticing her pink mouth again, how deep brown her eyes were, and he wondered, just briefly, what it would feel like to run his fingers through all that lush hair.

Uh-oh. *Okay, out the door, Dawson. Now.* Today had been long—his first official day at Dawson Solutions—and he was clearly tired. He couldn't possibly be thinking of Molly in a sexual way: a) that would be wrong, and b) he was in love with her best friend. He tried to picture Danica, but for some reason, Lucy and her llama book kept floating into his head.

He definitely needed a good night's sleep.

As Molly slid through her pantsuits in her closet, searching for the perfect second-day-at-work outfit, she couldn't stop thinking about the way Zeke had looked at her a few times earlier tonight—as though he *wanted* her. Wanted to kiss her. Wanted to carry her off to bed. Molly hadn't been the recipient of that look very often in her thirty-one years. And she'd been so surprised—completely caught off guard, really—that she'd almost choked on her slice of cake.

Could Zeke Dawson, man of her dreams since age twelve, tall, dark and impossibly gorgeous, have been looking at her with desire? She'd seen the smolder in his blue eyes, particularly as his gaze had dropped to her lips, where his eyes had lingered.

A slow, sweet smile lit across her face and she stared at herself in the full-length mirror on the inside of her closet door. She may not be a hot tamale but she wasn't chopped liver. One guy she'd dated in her early twenties had told her she had the prettiest brown eyes and would burst into that song by Van Morrison whenever they met for a date. She'd soon discovered he had a song for quite a few women at the same time, but still. Another guy, who'd ended up ghosting her, had told her he found her "inexplicably sexy" but she wasn't sure if that was a compliment.

Her ex-husband used to compliment her on individual features—her toned arms, the symmetry of her face, her feet that lacked corns or bunions.

But she couldn't recall him ever saying she was beautiful or sexy. They'd started out as friends and then began dating, though neither of them was particularly in love, and suddenly they were a couple. He was a bit older, thirty-five, and looking to settle down and he proposed by saying, *We should get married and start a family. I mean, we get along great, right? And that's what counts.*

And Molly had thought, *Well, it's not like Zeke Dawson is going to fall out of the sky and ask me to marry him, so why the hell not?* That was how Molly had found herself married to a perfectly fine guy with his own successful auto repair shop. They'd fallen into marriage instead of into love. Andrew had cried when he'd told her he'd unexpectedly found himself madly in love with his new ace mechanic, Lila, but it was so overpowering that, yes, he was going to break up his marriage to his newly pregnant wife. Molly had been devastated and furious and scared. But as time had passed, she began to understand if not exactly condone.

If Andrew could find his soul mate out of the blue, then who said anything wasn't possible? Zeke *had* fallen out of the sky, hadn't he? Right back in her path. That had to mean something.

And he *had* looked at her like he wanted to pick

her up in his arms, kiss her soap-opera style and carry her off to bed.

She smiled again, wondering if she should make her lips even more appealing to Zeke with a little gloss when her phone rang. Danica. Which reminded her. Would Zeke be looking at Molly with soap-opera lust when he had a serious crush on Danica?

Hmm. Maybe not. Maybe the whole thing had been her wishful thinking.

Molly plopped down on her bed and got comfy. "Tell me all about your first date back on the circuit!"

Was it selfish that Molly was hoping Danica had a great time with the bronc champ and that she couldn't wait to see him again? Okay, it was a little. But Danica would be happy *and* Molly wouldn't have to worry about her friend being free to date Zeke.

"Not only wasn't he a nice guy," Danica said, "he told me I should get myself a pair of black skinny jeans like our waitress had on in Ruby's Steakhouse after he complimented her on how good she looked in them right in front of me! What a jerk!"

Wait—what? Molly thought. *This kind of thing happens to women who looked like Danica?* How was that possible? Then again, she realized with a mental thunk to her forehead, Danica's husband had cheated on her. Beautiful women weren't immune.

"I can't believe he even noticed another woman while sitting across from you," Molly said. "That's nuts."

"Well, that's sweet of you to say but trust me, his eyes were all over every woman who walked by. Ugh. But you know what? The old Danica would have tried to win his attention. The new Danica told him he'd given her a headache before the dessert menu arrived and left."

"Yes! Good for you, Danica! But sorry he was an idiot. There are good guys out there. I really believe that."

"I sure hope so. Tomorrow night right after work I'm having coffee with a dentist. He has a great smile. We'll see. So tell me how your first day at your new job was! Your boss seems so nice and polite—nothing like that troll of a last boss. I don't really remember him from high school, though I remember all the Dawson boys were very cute. In fact, I sold a house to a Dawson just the other day—Ford. Talk about oil and water, but hey, I did get the sale."

Maybe Danica would be oil and water with

Molly's Dawson. Not that she wanted her friend to think Zeke was anything less than amazing. Sometimes, all this nonsense got complicated.

"Zeke is wonderful," Molly said, catching the dreamy quality in her voice and hoping Danica didn't. She cleared her throat. "He's very kind and the work he does is so interesting. Helping companies find solutions to their problems, whether financial or with employees."

"I'm so happy for you, Molly. And it doesn't hurt that he's so attractive."

Molly swallowed. Of course Danica found Zeke attractive. Any woman would.

She was dying to tell her bestie every last detail—how much she wanted to kiss Zeke, the way he was with Lucy, the real bond developing between them—and to talk about whether or not she was imagining that smoldering look in his eyes. But the words just wouldn't come out. Should she tell Danica *everything*? About her long-term crush on Zeke? About his long-term crush on Danica and how he was getting advice from Molly about winning her over? The whole thing would make Danica uncomfortable and put her in a funny position since her friend would know that had to hurt Molly and was compounded by Zeke being Molly's boss. So she couldn't say a word. She'd just have to see how it all played out.

Molly had been putting too much stock in the bronc champ, hoping he'd be great and that Danica would fall for him so that she'd be off the market again. Then at least Molly would have more time for her and Zeke's clear chemistry to lead him to notice her as a woman. She was half sure that was what had been going on earlier tonight. So pipe dream or not, she was going glass half full on the pursuit of Zeke Dawson. Didn't she intend to teach Lucy to reach for the stars?

Zeke liked her—a lot. She knew that, could feel it. And the more a person liked someone, the more attractive that someone became, right? In a month, Zeke might look at Molly and see Cindy Crawford in her Pepsi commercial. She bit her lip, realizing that was exactly what she wanted. For Zeke to fall for her because he saw her as beautiful on the inside *and* outside—by being herself.

But come on. All the confidence in the world wouldn't make Molly the kind of woman Zeke went for: a woman who looked like Danica. Was this pointless or not?

She got up and went to the mirror and studied herself. Wild mess of hair in a lopsided bun. Not a shred of makeup. Unpolished short nails—and toes. Plain old Molly Orton.

"Danica, do you think I should get a makeover?" Molly asked. "Be more glam? Straighten my hair? Wear less conservative clothes?" She needed a fairy godmother. Wyoming Cinderella—that was Molly.

"What on earth for?"

"To get my Mr. Right," Molly said. "You know the luck I had on the Converse County Singles app. Maybe I should present myself as more of what men want on the surface."

"No way. You're not looking for surface, Molly. You want the real deal. Your Mr. Right will love you the way *are*. The real you. So no. You don't need keratin treatments or a pencil skirt."

Molly gave a sigh of resignation, closed her closet and flopped back on her bed. "I'm glad you said that because I can't imagine spending a half hour on my makeup and hair every morning or trying to sit down in a tight skirt. That's definitely not me."

"I spend over an hour of my morning on hair and makeup, Molly," Danica said on a laugh. "But I love all that, including my five-step skin care routine and my two primers before I even apply my foundation and my spray mist to help set my finished face. I like my high heels. And I'm used to being slightly uncomfortable in my clothes and shoes. But I'm supergirlie—that's me. I don't do it to attract attention. I do it because I like it. I remember being five, six years old and watching my mom get all dolled up for work and evenings out with my dad and I couldn't wait to get my own perfume atomizer and powder puff."

Okay, she could see that. All of it. But where did that leave Molly? "And I do absolutely nothing because I like being invisible and fading into the woodwork?" That couldn't be right. She thought of her various-shades-of-beige pantsuits and sensible, neutral-colored shoes and frowned. Maybe it was. She'd never liked standing out or being the center of attention—even on her wedding day.

"First of all, Molly Orton, you're not invisible. Yesterday at work, one of the Realtors said to me, 'Can you ask your friend with the gorgeous curly hair where she gets it cut?'"

"Really? That's nice to know." Huh. "And I got it done at Dream Hair near the bakery."

"I'll let her know. And you *don't* fade into the woodwork," Danica added. "Your style is natural and conservative. That's always been you, and why is flashy and tight better? It's not. Remember when you tried mascara in sixth grade and were miserable until you washed it off? To be honest, I've always envied that, that the real you is front and center all the time. I wear makeup to the health club, Molly."

She laughed. "So I guess we're both just us."

"Right! Team Us. And the new and stronger Danica doesn't date jerks who ogle waitresses."

"Yeah! And the new and stronger Molly goes for what she wants."

And what she wants is Zeke Dawson.

By the time they hung up, Molly was set on this new path of getting Zeke Dawson by just being herself. She'd be her *own* fairy godmother.

Chapter Five

Once again, Zeke beat Molly to work on Tuesday morning, and had not only made the coffee but had brought in croissants—superflaky and buttery—and left them at the coffee station with a sticky note that read, *Help yourself.*

I would like to help myself to you, Molly thought as he came out of his office in a sharp and sexy dark blue suit. They made some brief chitchat and then got down to business; she knew he had a busy morning—two meetings with presentations since she was the keeper of his schedule. He gave her a heap of work to get through by noon—research into two companies in the county—but as he stood close, explaining what he wanted, the scent of his soap and shampoo driving her wild at 8:52 a.m., she'd assured him she'd make it happen. She'd gotten a killer smile in return.

By 11:40, she was done, her report ready to be emailed and the hard copy dropped off in his office. She'd wanted to be finished before he arrived back from his final meeting of the morning so that he'd return to her wonderful efficiency. Hey, it all added up.

She'd just returned to her desk with a satisfied smile when the office phone rang.

"Dawson Solutions, Inc., how may I help you?"

"Good morning," said a very familiar voice. "I'd like to make an appointment with Mr. Dawson."

"Dad?" Molly asked, tilting her head.

"Well, yes, sweetheart, but I'm calling as Tim Orton, owner of Tim's Tasty Tacos."

But why? Her father had said business at his new food truck was booming and that he was on his way to recouping his initial output—a chunk of her parents' retirement—and making a profit in only two weeks. Why would he want to meet with a consultant who turned failing companies around? Unless…

"Dad, I mean Tim, is everything okay?"

He didn't respond for a few seconds, then she heard the sigh in his voice. "Every day since my grand opening I've sold fewer and fewer tacos. Yesterday, five. Five, Molly! I can eat five of my tacos in *one* sitting. I just don't get it! So I'd like to make an appointment with Zeke Dawson to help me figure out what I'm doing wrong. Oh, and, Molly? I haven't mentioned sales or lack thereof to your mother yet. I just smile and say, 'Great!' when she asks how things are going, so maybe we can keep this between us for a bit? Just until I start to turn things around so she doesn't worry."

Oh, dear.

Molly's father had retired three months ago from the IT department of the hospital in Prairie City and though he hadn't exactly loved his job, he'd been so miserable puttering around the house that Molly's mom had suggested he follow his heart—the career choice he'd put aside "to be practical as a young married man." Cooking. Except Abby Orton had been talking about a part-time job as a short-order cook at the diner, whipping up chocolate chip pancakes and bacon cheeseburgers and making BLTs.

But Tim Orton didn't have any experience to get him a cooking job and he'd been getting more and more dejected and bored. So when he noticed busy food trucks in Prairie City, he lit on the idea of opening his own—selling tacos and only tacos, his favorite food. His wife had been understandably nervous. What did he know about the food truck business? He'd assured Abby he'd do his research and wouldn't use too much of their savings to buy the truck and that he'd be such a hit that they'd make back the investment within a month. That clearly wasn't happening. Molly had been a lot more enthusiastic and supportive than her very practical mother over the new venture. After all, who didn't love tacos? And her dad's idea to park the truck in Prairie City, a much larger, more bustling town, seemed like solid business sense, even if she couldn't drive the hour total there and back for tacos on her lunch break.

She was about to tell her father that she'd have Zeke return his call when the man himself returned to the office. Molly offered Zeke a smile as he took off his charcoal overcoat and hung it up. "Dad, I'll let Zeke know you'd like to set up a meeting—"

Zeke did a double take. "Your father? Put him through to my office."

Of course that was his response. Because he was great.

"Dad, hang on for a sec. Zeke will be right with you."

"Oh, thank heavens," Tim Orton said, relief coating his voice. "Love you, Molly-cakes."

"Love you, too, Dad." She transferred the call and replaced the receiver, wishing she could eavesdrop.

Sure was something for her boss to drop everything to talk to her dad the second he walked in after two meetings with clients. Zeke had done that for her, she knew, and a warm burst of gooey joy spread inside her chest, filling every little nook and cranny of her heart. Zeke was the definition of a good person. She knew from his schedule that he had a busy afternoon planned—working on strategy for two of his new clients with her at the ready to do any pop-up research on the companies, rivals and tactics, chasing down intel, researching stats. In fact, the entire week was pretty packed with client meetings, strategy and presentations. She wasn't sure when he'd be able to actually sit down with her father for a face-to-face meeting about the taco truck.

A few minutes later, Zeke was back. "You can start a New Client file for Tim Orton, proprietor of Tim's Tasty Tacos." He smiled and reached for his coat, shrugging into it. "I'm heading out to Prairie City to meet with him at the truck now."

She almost fell off her chair. "Oh, Zeke, you don't need to do that because he's my dad—I know you were planning to work on the Miller and Ranelli accounts this afternoon."

"Client needs me, I'm there," he said. "That's the Dawson Solutions way. I could hear the worry in your father's voice, as I'm sure you did—and yes, that he's your dad means he gets special treatment. That's the *Dawson* way."

Why do you have be so damned good and generous on top of being gorgeous?

"Besides," Zeke continued, "in that two-minute conversation I was able to note three major problems with the truck, so I have a feeling we'll have Tim's Tasty Tacos out of the red in no time."

Oh, Zeke. Could you be any more wonderful? "I appreciate that. He did sound very worried."

"We'll turn it around. That's what I'm here for." He laid a warm strong hand on her shoulder, then added, "I was going to pop into Danica's realty office today to talk houses but that can wait till later or tomorrow. I *am* in the market, and I figure while she and I are discussing homes, I can get a sense of whether I should ask her out or not or hold off.

Thanks to your tips, I have on my blue shirt and know not to make juvenile jokes. Not that I would."

She really did try to smile but couldn't get it to stretch very far. Ugh. She'd noticed the blue shirt because it brought out his eyes, and the bit of it she could see against his muscular chest under his suit jacket had her wondering if he had a hairy chest or if it was bare and smooth. But she hadn't related it to her advice about Danica's favorite color.

Because you very foolishly thought he was into you last night. Looking at you like he'd look at Danica. Wanting you like he wanted her. Dummy, she told herself, a little nook of her heart unfilling with that warm goo from just a little while ago.

She mentally shook her head at herself. *You've never been a daydreamer, Molly. Don't start now when it'll lead to a smashed heart and have you so off balance you'll be bad at your job and get fired.*

"Yeah, I'm thinking that'll have to wait till tomorrow," he added on a nod. "Guess I'll have to pick a blue tie for Wednesday." He shot her his dazzling smile, buttoning up his coat.

A day's reprieve from getting a call from Danica, her friend excitedly telling Molly that Zeke had come in to talk about available houses in Bear Ridge and he asked her out and *Gosh, I'd love to say yes but would you find that weird or con-*

flict of interest-y if your BFF started dating your boss, Mols?

Danica *would* ask because she, too, was great, and she would consider Molly before herself.

Blast it. Danica and Zeke were so damned thoughtful they *did* belong together.

Get it together, Molly. They're not a pair. Yeah, they're both nice. That's pretty much all they have in common besides both being gorgeous, too. They'd have no chemistry—Molly was sure of that.

Okay, phew. Heart rate back to normal. And his week was so busy that maybe he wouldn't have time to stop in at the realty. Danica was always in and out, too, so it was possible "stopping in" wouldn't work out. Double phew.

"Thanks again for dropping everything to help my father," she said, her mind turning to Tim Orton. She suddenly pictured him in his truck, thousands of taco shells and heads of lettuce piling up and no money in the till. She bit her lip, wishing she could join in on the meeting, rush to her dad's side and help, but he was getting an expert.

"It's my pleasure," he said. "Oh, and normally you'd be privy to all client communication, but since this is your family and your father might want to keep it private from his daughter, who happens to be my admin, I'll respect his wishes. But if he's comfortable with you knowing the details, I'll bring you in on the case. Knowing your dad the way you do could be a real help when I get into the personal nitty-gritty of why the truck is underperforming."

She tilted her head. "*Personal* nitty-gritty?"

"Sometimes people want to fail without realizing it—for many surprising reasons. So sometimes I have to deal with that issue first before coming up with restructuring solutions."

"Huh. That's interesting. In a sad way, I mean. I'm not sure that sounds like my dad, but I'm glad he's getting you, Zeke."

"Of course. I also won't be billing him, so no worries there."

Her eyes widened. "Wait—what? He's a client." She knew what Zeke billed per hour. He didn't come cheap. Two free hours of his time was a lot. But it wasn't like her father had more money to spend on this business right now.

The dazzling smile was back. "He's your dad. End of story." He glanced at his watch and before she could say anything, he added, "I'd better get going. See you later." And was out the door.

Molly had thought she was in love with Zeke

Dawson before? This generosity to her, to her family, tipped her over into another realm entirely. So now she had *epic* love for a man in love with someone else? Her best friend, no less?

Even if Danica wasn't a factor, there was the matter of Zeke not wanting to be a family man, to have kids. And Molly was a package deal. Love her, love her little girl, love all things family. Then again, as he'd said, the right woman could turn that around.

She glanced out the window just in time to see Zeke getting into his car parked a few doors down, almost in front of Bear Ridge Realty. There'd been two spots right in front of Dawson Solutions when she'd arrived; she'd taken one and recalled how she'd been surprised to find he was already in the office since he hadn't parked two feet from the door. There was a spot available in front now, too. He'd obviously parked in front of Danica's office to up the chances of "running into her" every time he went to his car. Realtors were constantly coming and going. So was the busy consultant.

Epic heartache was on the way, like a bullet train when she was positioned on the tracks way up ahead, knowing it was coming fast and unable to do anything about it.

* * *

The one thing that wasn't wrong with Tim's Tasty Tacos? The tacos. Delicious. Zeke sat on a little round stool by the large window where Tim Orton took and served orders—not that he'd taken or served any in the thirty minutes Zeke had been here. In that time, two people had approached the truck. One to ask Tim if he had swordfish tacos— no, he did not, sorry—and another to ask where the spin studio was. Two doors down.

It was prime lunchtime, too: 12:50. The truck should have a line of folks.

As Tim cleaned the already spotless stainless-steel counter, Zeke could see the family resemblance to Molly in the man's worried face—and in the brown curls poking out from under his Wyoming Cowboys baseball cap. Tim was tall and wiry with an open, warm face and easy smile.

"The good news is that the tacos are delicious," Zeke said, crumbling up his napkin and putting it in the cardboard tray his lunch had been served in. "The ground beef was seasoned perfectly, the lettuce crisp, the cheese fresh and the salsa just right. But here's a basic rundown of what I've noticed could be impeding business."

Tim, clearly eager to hear, sat on the stool across

from Zeke. He pulled out a small notebook from his shirt pocket and a tiny pen. "Ready."

"Number one," Zeke said. "Location, location, location. I'm sure there's a reason you chose to park in front of a playground full of snow that gets no visitors or foot traffic."

Prairie City had a vibrant two-mile long shopping district with side streets full of interesting shops and townhomes. Yet the truck was parked at the tail end of the shopping area and across the road where there was a small park that no one visited in February. A food truck in winter could work because the orders were quick and to go. But surely Tim had to know location was everything.

"Well, the city council people gave me a few options for location," Tim said. "I thought the park would still attract people since it cuts through a residential neighborhood on the other side. But yeah, I suppose I could park in one of the other two spots I was offered. One is in front of the library and the other is up at the start of Prairie Avenue by the big health club."

"Near the health club is a juice bar and a big yoga studio. Unless you're serving tofu tacos in kale wraps, I'd avoid that spot, too."

Tim laughed and looked hopeful, that at least he hadn't picked *that* option.

"Now, over by the library sounds like a solid location." Zeke pulled out his phone and brought up the library on his map app, including nearby shops.

"But there are so many options for food there," Tim countered. "That great fish-and-chips place. A bar and grill. That terrific little Italian bistro. The Chinese restaurant."

"Yet no Mexican food," Zeke said.

Tim tapped his pen against his chin. "Huh. Good point."

"Aside from the places you mentioned, there's a coffee bar, a bookstore and the movie theater right around there. Now, when folks come out of the latest Marvel movie, for which they spent a small fortune on tickets and popcorn and soda and Milk Duds, they might want to go less expensive for dinner. So they're going to be excited about the taco truck. Which brings us to point number two."

Tim had his pen ready again.

"Tacos are small-ish and get eaten in about six bites," Zeke said. "Six bucks for a six-bite item, especially from a food truck where the quick to-go factor is a huge draw, is too high. Even five is too high. Four dollars—just right. Most people will order two tacos, hand you ten bucks and get change. People like change. And you want to come in less expensive than the fish-and-chips place, which offers a take-out menu where most things are ten bucks or more."

"Oh, this is gold." Tim was nodding slowly. "I think you're onto something there."

"And gathering spots like the coffee bar and bookstore will have foot traffic all day, your tacos providing the perfect lunch, dinner or snack at an affordable price."

"I'll move today," Tim said, jotting down notes. "And will make a new menu board with my prices."

Zeke nodded. He was glad that Tim didn't seem to be in the "wanting to fail without realizing it" camp—that would make success all the more easier. "Which brings up point three. The menu board. You offer one kind of taco and one kind only."

"That's right. Ground beef tacos with cheese, lettuce and a great mild chunky salsa. The standard and most popular. Plus, by serving one kind, I can take the order, assemble the tacos in five seconds because there's no thinking involved, and serve the customer. That lets me be an efficient one-man show."

"I do like ground beef tacos," Zeke said. "They remind me of childhood. And people do like to be reminded of childhood even when those weren't the best of times. But *my* favorite? Shredded pork. My brother Ford isn't much of a meat eater and always

gets black bean dishes at Mexican restaurants—
he'd want black bean tacos with chunky hot salsa.
My sister loves chicken tacos with medium salsa.
My nephew Danny? Fish tacos—believe it or not.
Haddock, cod—with no salsa, no nothing actually.
And I know all this because we went to Margarita's
Mexican last week for the Taco Tuesday special.
Oh—and that guy who stopped by earlier? He
wanted swordfish."

Tim's eyes widened. "Swordfish costs a fortune."

"True. But haddock or cod doesn't, and if he'd
seen either of those are the menu, he might have
ordered. I'm thinking you could offer five kinds
of tacos. You'll need a helper, especially because
you're going to get very busy. But even paying an
employee you'll still come out way ahead with
all these changes. Make the menu board easier to
read and more colorful, offer a daily special and
all I've said so far is a solid start to attracting a
huge customer base."

Tim brightened. "I'll ask my wife if she wants
to come aboard. We can take turns with all the
various jobs in the truck. We'd be equal partners.
I think we'd both enjoy that very much. Partners
in business and life."

Zeke liked Tim Orton. "Sounds great to me."

"No one knows about that better than you and your family," Tim said. "First your grandparents were partners in running the guest ranch, then your dad with his wife."

You mean wives.

Zeke had a sudden memory jolt of his step-mother, Leah Dawson, Noah and Daisy's mother, telling his father they needed to be partners on the ranch if they were going to get it back to its glory days. Bo had actually told Leah "not to worry her pretty little head about all that," and she'd given him an earful about condescending to her and if he didn't start listening he'd run the place into the ground. It was pretty much there, at that point, that Bo was drinking his workers' paychecks and any profits.

Zeke and his brothers had learned how not to treat women by watching their father. Of course, commitment had never been any trouble for Bo Dawson; he'd committed easily and often, but the word hadn't meant much. Zeke had learned early on that committing only to his work meant he'd never let anyone down. No one was waiting up for him. No dashed expectations or hopes. Family wouldn't interfere with business. Business wouldn't interfere with family.

"And now the next generation of Dawsons are

running the place—isn't that something?" Tim added, his voice wistful. "I'll tell you, Zeke. One of the reasons I wanted to have this food truck wasn't just to keep busy. I see this as an investment in Molly's and that cute little Lucy's future. All the proceeds will go straight into what I call their 'future fund,' whether that's Molly having the down payment for a house of her own instead of a rental, or a college fund for Lucy."

Zeke felt something shift in his chest, something hard. What he'd have given for his own father to have felt that way, to have considered his children and future grandchildren with how he handled himself and the ranch. Instead, Bo Dawson had trampled on everything he'd supposedly loved.

"Your dad would be so proud of you all," Tim said, pride in his voice. "I didn't know Bo well, but we were in school at the same time and he was everyone's friend, got all the girls." He smiled. "I know he had his troubles but he would be proud."

Zeke managed a smile. "Maybe. I don't know. He wasn't exactly focused on the future. I don't think he wanted anything for us."

He hoped Molly knew how lucky she was to have a dad like Tim. He had a feeling she did.

"Oh, fathers always do," Tim said, "even if

they're not going to win any parenting awards. I'm sure he cared deeply about you six even if in his own way."

Zeke thought about the letters his father had left all his kids. Bo hadn't had much to his name—the ramshackle ranch itself, his personal possessions, which amounted to broken furniture he hadn't been able to sell to support his drinking and gambling, and some of his parents' things in the attic, which Zeke and his siblings were relieved to see Bo hadn't sold. Some things were keepsakes, even to Bo—like Noah and Daisy's late mother's wedding rings, which he could have sold but instead saved for Daisy and left them to her in the bequeathment letter. That had meant the world to his sister.

In the letter he'd left Zeke, Bo had said he had no idea how he'd gotten a business whiz for a kid but one of his brothers had sent him a local magazine with a big write-up about Zeke, mover and shaker in Cheyenne, and Bo would sure appreciate knowing that Zeke would use his "financial smarts" to get the ranch back in the black.

Of course, back then, two Christmases ago, none of the Dawsons had expected to rebuild the ranch. Once they'd all committed—though only Noah and Daisy had been willing back then to ac-

tually live at the ranch and take on the project—
Zeke had handled the business and financials with
Noah long-distance. Last summer, the ranch had
reopened Memorial Day weekend for the first time
in ten years and was an instant hit. Slowly, all the
siblings came home and Zeke still operated as the
unofficial chief financial officer, handling the big
picture while Noah and his forewoman wife, Sara,
took care of the day to day. Zeke felt good about
helping out with the ranch; his father had asked
from the grave, and Zeke had complied, and that
gave him a certain measure of peace.

"And of course I'd love to get Molly's opinion
on the new menu, especially," Tim said. "Molly
loves tacos like crazy."

He thought of the swordfish tacos she'd ordered
on her first day at Dawson Solutions. "She's fabu-
lous, our Molly," Zeke said.

The *our Molly* had come out of his mouth before
he'd thought about it—and Zeke usually measured
his words carefully. Then again, she certainly did
feel like *his* Molly.

Tim beamed. "Oh, she sure is. She's a real trouper.
One of the strongest people I know. As dependable
as the rising and setting sun."

And lovely, too. Inside and out, Zeke thought as
her face came to mind, her expressive brown eyes,

the wild dark curls falling past her shoulders. He stood. "Why don't you wrap up four tacos for the road? Two for Molly and two more for me. It's almost a good thing you're out here in Prairie City or I'd come by the truck a couple times a day and have to add a half hour to my daily workout." He pulled out this wallet.

Tim held up a hand. "Are you kidding? On the house. And who knows? Maybe Tim's Tasty Tacos will get so popular we'll have another truck in Bear Ridge one day."

Zeke smiled and put his wallet away. "Think big. I like it."

Tim stood up and headed over to the taco station. "Nice of you to think of Molly, by the way. Tell her I put lots of salsa on hers. She loves the stuff."

"I will, Tim. And feel free to call or email or text with any questions. I'm here for you as a sounding board with details and the big picture. Any time. And my services are also on the house. I insist."

Surprise lit up Tim's face and he extended his hand, giving it a hearty, appreciative shake. "You're all right, Zeke Dawson."

For a moment, it was as if his own father had said those words with that beaming expression, and they slid right inside Zeke's cells. He hadn't realized how much the fatherly approval would mean.

But these days, Zeke was constantly getting surprised.

Chapter Six

On Saturday morning, Molly woke up almost relieved that it wasn't a workday. She'd made it through five days of working with Zeke, being a vital part of his business. Every morning she'd arrived at the office with a big piece of her "switched off" so that she could be professional and get her work done and not just stare like the dreamy-eyed high-schooler she used to be, making hearts with their initials on it. That got harder and harder the more she got to know him, particularly after her father had called her singing Zeke's praises about how he'd singlehandedly saved all of their futures and wasn't charging him a penny. In the days following his meeting with Zeke, her dad had texted her at least three times a day with how brilliant, generous and wonderful Zeke Dawson was.

It had taken a lot for Molly not to say, *I know, right?* with a giant sigh, and dish to her father about how in love with the man she was. She and her dad were close but she wasn't ready to let anyone know how she felt about Zeke. She probably never would be.

That way, no one would even guess that she was practically jumping out of her skin with excitement about tomorrow—when she and Lucy would be visiting the Dawson Family Guest Ranch with Zeke as their personal tour guide. The forecast called for fifty degrees, which was springlike in Wyoming in February. A day at the ranch, visiting the petting zoo, having lunch in the cafeteria, a hike up Clover Mountain just the three of them—no business, all personal. Molly couldn't wait. Every day, the notion that something could develop between them seemed a possibility.

And she was grateful to be busy today. A cousin was babysitting Lucy for a few hours this morning while Molly and her parents worked on the new menu for Tim's Tasty Tacos. Her dad had spent the previous few days solidifying his ideas, and now the three of them were in the Ortons' kitchen, recipes on index cards handed down for generations scattered on the counter next to Molly's iPad to keep track of what the truck would offer.

"I'll tell you," Tim said, looking at a recipe yellowed with age for jerk chicken, "if Zeke Dawson had handed me an invoice for half a million dollars for his services, I wouldn't have blinked an eye. Not that I could pay it, just that everything he said the other day was worth that."

A puff of pride lit up inside Molly. "He's definitely good at what he does."

"And I liked how he thought of you and asked for tacos to bring back to the office," Tim added. "After that last horror of a boss, you deserve a prince like this, Molly-girl."

"And so handsome," Abby Orton said with a sly smile. "Any romance in the air?"

"Mom!" Molly said. "Of course not. That wouldn't be professional."

"Oh, please," Abby said. "Who can stop love?"

Molly laughed. "Um, Mom, he's my boss. And come on. He's as handsome as you say. And very successful. And very nice. He can have his pick of single women and there are plenty of beauties in town."

Like Danica.

"Right, including you," Tim said. "You're the most beautiful gal in Bear Ridge, if you ask me. Next to your mother, of course."

Abby smiled. "Good save, Tim."

Molly mock-rolled her eyes. "I'm no Danica. Come on. Better to be realistic than dream of something that's never—"

Molly clamped her mouth shut. She hadn't meant to say any of that. She stared at the recipe card, all too aware of her parents' eyes on her. They were no fools.

"Danica is beautiful and so are you, Molly," her mother said, giving her daughter's chin a gentle tug.

Yeah, yeah, Molly thought, grateful that her parents were such sweethearts but rummaging through the recipe cards to feign concentration so they'd get back to the menu board. "So, Dad, I'm in complete agreement with your plan. The truck will offer five different tacos daily, enough to lure in all tastes, but not too complicated that they slow production. Ground beef tacos in your special seasoning, shredded pork marinated in that incredible chipotle sauce, black bean with a kick of spice, chunky chicken and pan-seared haddock. The big menu board will feature mouthwatering descriptions. You can change the 'special' every day and charge a dollar less per taco for that one."

"Sounds like a great plan to me," her mom said. "I'm so excited about my new role!" Molly's mother had been a math teacher for years before she retired, and she was taking on the business and financial end and "window gal," since she was so naturally friendly and patient. Molly's dad was a chitchatter, too, but he'd always been the chef of the family and wanted to focus on the food. And Molly would serve as sounding board and taco tester.

Her cell phone rang and she grabbed it. *Please don't be Zeke canceling tomorrow,* she thought. She wanted that day—*needed* that day.

It was Danica. "Hi, hon. I owe you one. Your boss just called to set up a meeting with me for Monday morning. He's looking for a house in town. Thanks for sending a new client—especially one with that kind of budget—my way!"

Molly's heart dropped straight to her stomach. *Except I didn't. And wouldn't.* First of all, Zeke already knew his dream woman was a Realtor and his own brother had been a satisfied client. So it wasn't like Molly was a bad friend for not handing over her BFF's card and suggesting he call her. But Danica thought Molly did. Which her friend would take as Molly giving her blessing for the two of them to date.

Oh, foo. This was where it would start between Danica and Zeke. A meeting. Extending to lunch. Then dinner. Then bed. Then an excited call from Danica in the morning. Then Molly, crying.

"How was last night's date?" Molly asked.

"Another no," Danica said on a sigh. "A few things jumped out at me that wouldn't have until you gave it to me straight."

Molly smiled. "Like what?"

"He was telling me that his dad has a riverfront cabin and that the two of them love to go ice fishing but then he referred to his stepmother as a 'royal bitch' who was always throwing roadblocks into their trips. I mean, maybe the stepmother is a terrible person. But who refers to his father's wife that way?"

"Ugh. And on a first date?"

"Next!" Danica said on a laugh.

Please, please, please, don't let Zeke be next.

"You're doing great, Danica. You'll find your dream guy."

"We *both* will. Oh, there's my two o'clock. Talk later."

Now Molly felt like she had tomorrow and only tomorrow to make Zeke fall madly in love with her before Monday, when he'd meet with Danica and end up proposing to her by week's end.

She pocketed her phone and turned her attention back to her parents and the taco menu. If only she could change her own life as easily as she could erase a whiteboard.

At home that night, Molly was trying one of the black bean tacos her dad had sent her home with when her phone pinged with a text.

Zeke.

Your dad texted that he had the menu board ready to go and wanted me to look it over. Said it's with you because you have the best handwriting in the fam. Good time to stop over?

Score one for Dad.

She texted back: Yes! And be hungry. Lots of trial tacos here.

Always hungry for tacos. See you soon.

Her heart soared and she raced into her bedroom and stared at herself in the full-length mirror. Bye, grubby jeans and blah long-sleeved T-shirt. She pulled on what Danica referred to as her long "slinky black sweater" and heather-gray leggings, then dabbed on a tiny bit of light perfume and put her hair up in a loose bun. Better.

She checked on Lucy, who was fast asleep in her crib, then headed downstairs, fluffing the sofa pillows and grabbing a few of Lucy's toys off the living room rug, and then just waited, so aware of her heightened expectations that she had to sit down.

I have tonight. I have tomorrow. Anything can happen. Anything is possible.

There was a rap on the door, and Zeke came in with yet another bakery box.

"Tres leches cake," he said, holding up the white box with the red ribbon. "To keep with the Mexican theme."

She could barely drag her eyes off him. He wore a black leather jacket, dark jeans, cowboy boots and a black Stetson. "Tres leches," she repeated, trying to remember her high school Spanish. "Three..." she prompted, closing the door behind him.

"Milks. With a delicious-looking frosting."

"Thanks, Zeke. You always come bearing gifts."

"It's the uncle in me. Like I'd ever show up without toys for my nieces and nephews when I visit any of my siblings? Well, except Ford."

"Ah, yes, the other holdout," she said, recalling him describing himself and Ford that way on the topic of marriage and children—within five minutes of his arrival the morning of her interview.

That was how strong the I-don't-want-to-be-a-father force was in him.

He didn't respond as she led the way into the kitchen. She wanted to pepper him with questions. He'd said the right woman could turn him around but she wasn't so sure about that. Wanting kids needed to come from the inside out, not the outside in. Ms. Right might change his mind about children because he was in love, but how would that make him less conflicted about being a father?

A heavy topic for another time. Not that she could imagine it coming up.

The whiteboard listing the menu was propped up on the kitchen table. She'd used multiple colors and very readable handwriting to make the board appealing and easy to read. It would definitely catch the attention of those walking along the main drag of Prairie City, deciding about lunch.

"What do you think?" she asked.

He walked closer, standing right beside her as he took in the menu board, reading the descriptions. He was so tantalizingly close. "Just perfect. The menu itself, the board itself. Who could resist any of this?"

Who indeed? she thought, the faint scent of his

soap in the air. "I'm so glad to hear that. My parents will be so relieved."

"Now I'm dying for a taco—any one of them."

She grinned. She just adored this guy. "I have shredded pork and chunky chicken," she said. "One of each?"

"Sold."

Molly sighed inwardly. She wanted him sold on *her*.

You have all day tomorrow, she reminded herself. And if Lucy's presence makes him realize he's right about his take on being a dad? Fine. Then he wasn't the man for her. His long hold on her would finally be over. Not that it would be so easy to get over giving up hope. But she was a package deal.

She got out the ingredients, heating up the chicken and pork in little saucepans on the stove, then warmed up the taco shells in the toaster oven. "I'll make them for you just as my dad would. Shredded lettuce, a combination of Monterey Jack and cotija cheeses and his medium slightly chunky secret salsa."

"Smells so good," he said, sniffing the air.

"I know! I can't resist—I'm about to have my third sampling."

He smiled and leaned against the counter, looking so sexy she almost dropped the plate of tacos as she brought them to the table.

She grabbed two bottles of beer from the fridge and then sat down. He took a chair across from her, a vase of short red tulips between them. *Almost like a date*, she thought, butterflies fluttering in her stomach.

"To Tim's Tasty Tacos," he said, holding up a taco.

Molly laughed and held up hers, too. They clinked them with a little flourish.

He took a bite, his expression letting her know he loved it. "Perfection. I can tell your dad clearly loves to cook. The seasoning and flavors—really delicious."

"Agreed," she said, finishing her bite. "So good!" She took a sip of her beer, then another bite. "I can't thank you enough for everything you've done for my parents. And me."

He looked at her with those gorgeous blue eyes and she almost swayed again. "My pleasure, really. Your parents are both great."

Her heart was about to overflow. "My mom told me she sees going into business with my dad as their thirty-third anniversary present. Originally it was going to be just his thing, but now that they're partners, they're both so excited. They were partners in life and now they're partners in business and can barely stop hugging each other in happiness."

"Thirty-three years," he repeated. "That's something."

Molly nodded. "They're high school sweethearts—met as freshmen. My dad saw my mom standing at her locker one day, chatting to a friend, and suddenly couldn't breathe or move. He worked up the courage to talk to her and they've been together ever since."

He held up his beer with a rueful smile. "That was my downfall—not working up the courage to talk to Danica. It was the same for me—I remember seeing her for the first time, also chatting with a friend, and I felt like I was zapped by lightning. I had to know this girl. But she had a boyfriend, then I had a girlfriend, then she had a boyfriend and we never got past hellos in a few classes."

Great to know, Molly thought, her heart plummeting to her toes. She'd completely forgotten her parents' story would remind him of his own experience. Why had she brought it up? Why, why, why?

"Funny to think that the friend she was talking

to was probably you," he said. "But there you have it. You've been there for two major events in my life. Seeing Danica for the first time. And opening Dawson Solutions."

"I'm sure it was me. Believe it or not, Danica didn't have a lot of friends in high school because she was *too* pretty. Isn't that crazy? People decided she was this or that solely based on how she looked."

He tilted his head, taking that in. "I guess I did, too. I decided she was meant for me just because of how she looks. Now that I think about it, in those terms, that's pretty shallow. But I guess that's how love at first sight works, teenager or adult."

"I know," she said before she could catch herself.

She could feel him watching her, the curiosity radiating off him.

"So you've experienced love at first sight?" he asked. "I guess everyone has at some point. Even those who seem more…"

She narrowed her eyes. "More what?"

"Practical. You don't seem like someone who'd get all wrapped up in looks—you'd go for personality, character."

"Well, I hate to burst your good opinion of me,

but it was love at first sight for me with someone in middle school." She felt a warm flush start in her stomach and trickle up to her face. "Not that he ever knew."

"Oh, yeah? Captain of the Mathletes?"

She gave him a playful punch on the arm. "What makes you think my crush wasn't a jock?"

"I can see you having a mad crush on someone really smart and focused. A student. Polite. Friendly to everyone. Am I right?"

"To be honest, I didn't get to know him well enough to even know if he was any of that."

"To love at first sight," he said, holding up his beer bottle.

No, no, no. To love at *real* sight. To love once you've gotten to know someone. Surely at this age, with the experience that came with it, he had to see that he didn't have real feelings for Danica just because she was gorgeous. She was in love with Zeke because he was gorgeous *and* wonderful.

"Well, I don't know about that toast," she said, keeping her bottle firmly on the table. "I mean, back then, of course you figured Danica was your dream girl just because you were wildly attracted. But now you must know the two of you could have zero chemistry, nothing to talk about, stilted conversations and

zilch in common. You could talk to her for five minutes and feel absolutely zippo."

"Well, I know that," he said. "But I doubt it."

"Because of the love-at-first-sight thing."

"It worked for your parents. And decades later,
they couldn't be happier."

He had her there. "I guess you're more of a romantic than I thought, Zeke. I mean, I'd call you
pragmatic and driven by reality, by what's what,
not fantasy. It's how you approach your work, I've
noticed. You deal with the facts of the situation."

"True. All I know is that my crush on her has
gotten me through some hard times in life."

She tilted her head. "What do you mean?"

"Back in school, when things with my father
were bad and they usually were, I'd see Danica in
the halls at school and I'd forget life at home. And
now, having just been burned by an ex and needing a fresh start somewhere else, I learn Danica
is single. Seems meant to be."

She bit her lip. She knew exactly what he was
talking about. Over the years, if she was feeling
down in the dumps and saw Zeke somewhere, her
mind would go from her troubles to how blue his
eyes were, how broad his shoulders, how completely dreamy he was. That went for fifteen years

ago and more recently—when she'd heard he was moving back to town.

"Sorry about the ex," she said. "I know what getting burned is like."

He nodded. "We're quite the pair, aren't we? A lot of heavy stuff in common." He popped the last of his taco in his mouth. "I can talk to you about anything. It's like the universe decided I'd had enough bad for a while and gave me a gift— a good friend and a terrific administrative assistant in one."

She did like being referred to as a gift. The friend part, not so much.

Though of course she treasured being his friend. His *good* friend. She just wanted much more.

"You know how my parents met?" he asked.

"How?"

"Because of tacos."

"What? Are you serious?"

He nodded. "Yup. Tacos clearly have deep meaning for us, Mol."

She grinned, waiting for him to continue, practically floating that he'd given her a nickname.

"My dad used to hang out at Margarita's Mexican restaurant," he said, "because Mondays through Wednesdays they had tacos for three for five bucks and draft beer was cheap. He fell in love with a waitress—Diana. My mom. She wouldn't give him the time of day at first because she'd seen him flirt with everyone—*and* how much he drank. But he wore her down by coming every day and working overtime to be her knight in shining armor."

"Three kids later…" she said with a smile.

"Yup. Marriage didn't last but I did get Rex and Axel out of it. Always had Ford, of course. Then along came Daisy and Noah when my dad remarried. And then there were six."

"I wish I had siblings," she said. "I have a great bunch of cousins, though, and we get together often."

"I know I'm lucky in the sibling department," he said. "Every one of them is the best person you'll meet."

"That's really nice, Zeke," she whispered, leaning a bit closer to him.

He smiled, looking at her intently, just inches separating them.

Kissable distance.

Her heart was beating—fast.

Her lips went dry.

The butterflies were flapping furiously.

Kiss me, kiss me, kiss me…

Suddenly the hair stick wedged into her bun

came loose and her curls fell down, tumbling and springing everywhere.

"I love your hair," he whispered, moving a long spiral from her cheek. He tucked it behind her ear. "It's so wild."

"Out of control," she whispered back.

He leaned closer.

She leaned closer.

And then their lips met and his hands were on her face, her mouth parting and his pressing harder. *Zeke, Zeke, Zeke. Oh, God, this is amazing. I'm dreaming. Someone pinch me. No, don't. Ohhh, Zeke...kiss me forever.*

Except he was pulling away. Dammit.

She opened her eyes to find him clearly upset, shaking his head.

"I don't know why I did that," he said, sitting very straight. "I assure you it'll never happen again. Just got carried away in the moment. I apologize, Molly."

It'll never happen again? Oh, yes, it would!

He bolted up. "Again, the menu is great and the reopening is right on target. I'd better get going. About tomorrow—"

"The petting zoo barn at one p.m.," she said

fast. *Please don't cancel. Please.* "I'm so excited to show Lucy the baby goats and all the animals."

She was. That wasn't a lie.

He seemed about to say something, then nodded as if realizing that maybe she was saving the day for him, getting them back to the way things were two minutes ago, when a day trip to his ranch as his assistant was perfectly okay, perfectly platonic. "See you then," he finally said, and quickly put on his jacket and hat.

He glanced at her with an awkward smile and then left.

Molly did a little dance, spinning around and throwing her hands up in the air.

He kissed me. Zeke Dawson kissed me.

He's attracted to me. He's falling for me.

He called me a gift!

No matter that he said the kiss would never happen again. That was the shock talking—at least she thought so, anyway. He'd surprised himself and beat the ole hasty retreat. More evidence that he'd been caught very off guard by his undeniable attraction to her. Molly Orton. The dependable plain Jane in pantsuits and floral scarves.

He'd kissed her because he wanted to. And that was all she needed to know.

And they'd be spending the fifty-degree afternoon together tomorrow, with her baby girl. Just like a couple.

This could actually happen, she thought. *I love you, Danica Dunbar, but this one is* mine.

Chapter Seven

Zeke had spent all night thinking about the kiss—and what it meant. He'd still be thinking about it right now, at eight thirty Sunday morning, but he was presently surrounded by children of all ages, and man, were they loud. He couldn't think if he'd tried.

He peered over the white railing that separated the infant area, where he stood, from the rest of the huge Kid Zone space in the ranch's lodge. Toddlers. Preschoolers. Big kids. Teens. They whipped around the room in happy shouts and giggles, sending foam balls into three-foot basketball hoops, building towers of blocks—his two-year-old nephew Danny was among those— coloring pictures, playing soccer, making crafts. Zeke's sister-in-law Maisey, head nanny of the ranch's babysitting service, had called him in a panic an hour ago—one of her employees had a family emergency and Maisey had a full house and no one was available. Could he spare two hours to keep an eye on the two sleeping babies, both his little relatives, if that made it less scary? It definitely did. So he'd donned the Dawson Family Guest Ranch staff polo shirt Maisey had presented him with and found himself spending the morning wondering how the babies slept so peacefully amid all the noise and action.

A little cry came from one of the babies—his sister's son, Tony, who was seven months old, but it was a false alarm and the little guy went right back to sleep. In the bassinet beside him was Maisey's daughter, eight-month-old Chloe. Maisey had said the little girl was a champion napper and she definitely was. A toddler let out a shriek that could crack glass, but Maisey didn't stir.

Tony, on the other hand? Suddenly screaming his little head off.

"Hey there, you're gonna wake up your cousin," Zeke said, lifting out his nephew and holding the baby against his chest. He gave Tony's back a rub and the tyke stopped crying and grabbed his ear instead. Ow. What was with babies and Zeke's ears?

Which of course made him think of Lucy, which made him think of Molly, which made him think of the way her lush hair had fallen down around her last night. Her hair, her face, her body, their ease of conversation, their laughter… He'd touched that curl and something inside him had given way. He'd wanted to kiss her, hold her, feel her against him.

Molly—his admin. Was he completely insane? Not okay, not appropriate. If they were coworkers on equal footing, fine. But he was her boss.

So now what? Even after just a week he knew she was a great admin, a great person, and he was damned lucky to have her, so he'd just better tamp down his attraction and somehow try to make it go away.

He shifted Tony in his arms, turning toward the two toddlers climbing a minimountain on a cushy mat so that the baby could have a fun view.

Last night, in his bed in the cabin that Ford had vacated, Zeke had tried hard to "make it go away." First, he'd berated himself for acting without thinking and just kissing her. Then he'd grabbed his high school yearbook and looked at Danica Dunbar's photo, waiting to feel that conk on the head, the bolt of lightning, the cartoon hearts shooting out of his chest as if he were Pepé Le Pew. Nothing.

And instead of planning his long-awaited date with Danica in his head—a great restaurant in Prairie City, him in a blue shirt—all he could think about was Molly. Molly sitting across from him, the little vase of red tulips between them. Clinking on tacos. Sharing stories. Touching that long, wild curl.

Wanting to kiss her. Wanting, wanting, wanting. And then doing so.

The more he'd looked at Danica's little square photo, the less connected to her, to the old dream, to the old him, he was. But he'd tried to focus, tried to remember how the thought of her would rally him. All so that he wouldn't be romantically interested in his administrative assistant. His good friend. The gift from the heavens.

What was he supposed to do with this? He'd just have to ignore his attraction. No other way. First of all, even if it was appropriate to kiss his subordinate, which it was not, Molly was a mother. A package deal. And Zeke wasn't meant for fatherhood.

"When are you going to make me an uncle?" said a familiar voice.

Zeke turned to find his brother Axel grinning at him. "You are an uncle. A few times over."

"Yeah, but look at you," Axel said, gently caressing Tony's light brown hair. "A natural."

Zeke raised an eyebrow. "No clue why. But babies do seem to love me."

"Well, babies did not seem to love me and I never thought I'd have kids—same as you. Then whammo—Danny, a missing toddler I rescued from a mountain—decides I'm his hero and suddenly I'm not only married to his mother but now we're expecting a baby."

How was this happening? Zeke wondered. One by one, all the Dawsons were changing diapers and singing lullabies, happily committed to the family life as if it was a natural next step. It wasn't. Not for any of them.

"There's something in the water," Axel added. "Turns commitment-phobes into family men walking around with babies in their arms and singing 'Itsy Bitsy Spider.' Like you were doing."

Had he been? He'd been so lost in thought he hadn't even realized.

"What is it, really?" Zeke asked. "I mean, I know there's not a magic potion in the water supply. So what is it? How did four out of six—so far—Dawsons end up married with kids?"

Axel was staring at his brother as though Zeke had grown an extra head. "Why do you sound like you're asking that seriously?"

Zeke narrowed his eyes at Axel. What was he missing here? "I am. So how?"

"Duh, bruh. It's a very simple concept. Maybe you've heard of it—love."

"So if I fall in love I'll magically want to be a dad?" Zeke asked. "Come on." Though that did seem to work for the rest of them.

"More like, if you fall in love, that thing in your chest expands in ways you never thought possible. Walls come crumbling down."

Well, he had figured the right woman could change his mind about having children, so this wasn't a new concept.

"Anyway," Axel added, "I'm here to relieve you. I'm back from leading a wilderness tour and have nothing planned for another hour, so you can take off if you want. And I'm figuring you want."

Zeke snuggled his baby nephew against his chest and kissed the top of his head. "I actually have some thinking to do and it's kind of loud in here. So I'll take you up on that."

The moment he transferred Tony into his

brother's arms, he missed the soft weight of him, the baby shampoo scent of his hair. God, what was happening to him?

"Watch out, guys!" Axel called over to a few preschoolers who were playing tag and were about to collide. Saved in the nick of time. "I've been filling in in the Kid Zone since last summer, and I never stop freaking out about kids getting hurt on my watch." He mock-shivered. "I wish they'd all sit and color. The teenagers, too."

"I'm trying to imagine Dad pinch-sitting at the Kid Zone for even fifteen minutes," Zeke said, his father's face, beer to his mouth, filling his mind.

"Yeah, I can't picture that, either. It's amazing how much we all look like Dad but none of us are like him."

Zeke stared at his brother. "Meaning what? How could we not be like him? He raised us."

"I'm not a negligent parent," Axel said. "I mean, here I am, worried about a foam soccer ball ending up smashing into someone's nose. We're all responsible, concerned people. Dad never worried about *anything*."

"I'm just being preemptive, then," Zeke said. "Not giving myself something to worry or not about. If that makes any sense."

"You think you're immune?" Axel asked. "Ha.

I thought I was, too. It'll get you. And when it does? You won't know what knocked you upside the head. Much harder than a foam soccer ball kicked by a four-year-old."

Kind of the way he felt now. Kicked upside the head. By his feelings for Molly Orton.

And in just a few hours, he'd be showing her and her baby around the petting zoo barn, laughing at the goats as they jumped on their logs, smiling at the piglets.

He'd cancel but he couldn't stop thinking of her expectant face as she'd confirmed the time last night. *One p.m. at the petting zoo...*

Zeke couldn't stop thinking of her face, period.

Molly couldn't take it. She wasn't going to confess to being in love with Zeke, but she had to ask Danica for advice on what to wear. It was forty-nine degrees, still cold even though not the usual freezing for February. Did she wear her big trusty puffy coat that gave her zero sex appeal? She had a camel-colored wool peacoat. Maybe that? But was that ranchy?

She called Danica. Her friend would think she just wanted to make a good impression on her boss. And she'd have perfect advice.

"Hmm, the puffy coat would keep you warm

on the tour for sure," Danica said. "But the peacoat has that more professional vibe and it's almost fifty, so I say the peacoat. And wear your cute flat brown boots—the knee-high ones. You have that one pair of dark skinny jeans that fit you so well. Wear those with any sweater that makes you feel happy and you're set."

Oooh, her skinny jeans generally stayed way to the side of her closet in favor of less "formfitting" ones. But they did look good on her. *Live a little, Molly!* "Okay, sounds good. And I was thinking the off-white cashmere my parents gave me for Christmas. Or is that too much for a petting zoo? I mean, this is dressy for me. But this *is* my boss *and* his whole family, really, so I do want to look nice."

"Cashmere is always a yes."

"Hair up or down?" Molly asked.

"Hmm, toughie. Normally I'd say up so that Lucy won't be grabbing at your curls but I love your hair when it's in all its loose glory."

So does Zeke, she thought, remembering the touch of his hand on her hair, on her face. A fluttering warmth gathered in her stomach.

Molly stared at her ho-hum face in her closet mirror. She'd always thought of it as a serviceable face, a perfectly nice face, but just nothing that would ever turn a head. And yet, this face, these ordinary features, had turned the head of the man of her dreams. She smiled, again remembering, almost able to feel the imprint of his warm, soft lips.

"Should I wear a little makeup?" Molly asked. "I do to the office, just a little powder and mascara so I don't look like I just rolled out of bed. But this is a Sunday afternoon at a dude ranch. I'll be petting goats and piglets."

"Either way sounds good to me. You can't go wrong with your unadorned pretty face or with a little polish."

Molly liked unadorned. But Zeke was used to seeing the slightly improved her from nine to five every day.

Hey, wait a minute. Last night, when Zeke had come over to check out the menu board, when he'd *kissed* her, she hadn't been wearing a stitch of makeup. She'd change her outfit and fluffed her hair, but there'd been no powder, no mascara. Just a little dab of her favorite solid perfume on her wrist.

And he'd seemed to like all that—all that nothing—just fine. She grinned, the warm flutter getting hotter.

Huh. She was her own fairy godmother, after all. Well, with a lot of help from her best friend.

"Your day sounds so nice—I know you'll have

a great time," Danica said. "I'm having a dog-walking date in the park with a welder named Jack. He seems great on the phone and the pics of his dog are so cute. Some kind of fluffy Australian shepherd. Oh, and the guy himself is pretty cute, too."

Please fall madly in love with Welder Jack so that you're too in love to even notice Zeke's blue eyes tomorrow at your Realtor meeting. Though would any woman not notice Zeke's gorgeousness? "Ooh, a cute dog guy. Sounds promising."

"I'll let you know. So far, every date has been a major fail on the nice meter."

Welder Jack, please be a mensch, Molly prayed to the fates of the universe. *The good guy Danica deserves. So we can both be happy!*

An hour later, in her Danica-approved outfit and bare face, hair loose, Lucy buckled into her car seat, Molly arrived at the Dawson Family Guest Ranch at a few minutes to one. Zeke had said he'd meet her just past the front gates at the Welcome Hut. And there he was, standing beside the cute green structure, waving at her as she drove in. He wore that sexy black leather jacket and Stetson, with jeans and cowboy boots.

He gestured her into a parking spot and came

over to the car. "No dogs, today, unfortunately. Both Dude and River are at the vet for checkups."

"Well, we'll have plenty of animal companions," she said, excited to see the piglets.

He nodded. "We can walk everywhere from here. What are you thinking—stroller, too, or just the chest carrier?"

Hmm, if he kissed her again, it would help to have Lucy in her stroller so that the baby didn't get smushed, right? "Definitely both."

He nodded, lugging out the stroller from the cargo area. Every time she didn't have to do that herself, she gave thanks. Of course, the only other time she wasn't doing the lugging was when she was with her dad.

"Hi, Lucy!" Zeke said as he unbuckled Lucy's harness and took her out. The baby stared at him. "You're gonna see the cutest goats today. And two alpacas. And sheep and piglets and cows and horses. And lots of land with snow covering the mountains beyond. There's no more beautiful place than right here."

"Ga ba!" Lucy said with a grin, grabbing Zeke's ear.

"Babies love my ears," he said as he put Lucy in the stroller and buckled her harness. "I thought it was me but it's just my ears they love."

Molly laughed. "Better you than me."

He reached toward her with an evil grin to pretend-grab at her ear, but he got her curls instead and practically turned white. "Sorry—trying to be funny and, here I am, touching you again."

Maybe he did mean what he'd said last night— that the kiss wouldn't happen again. That he wouldn't let it even if he wanted to.

Lighten the mood, Molly. Fast. "Hey, I get it. You can't resist this crazy mane." She gave it a shake, his eyes following the swish-swish.

"I can't," he said quietly. "That's a problem."

The breath whooshed right out of her. Had she heard that right? Was she dreaming? She knew *something* had shifted between them last night, something big, but given his reaction and the way he'd run out of her house, she'd figured he'd avoid any mention of the kiss.

"You can't resist this?" She grabbed gobfulls of the wild curls that had given her grief from age six when the bully sitting behind her in class would pull on them, to middle school when she dreamed of smooth, straight hair like most of the girls seemed to have.

Now is not the time to be cracking jokes, Molly. The man is being serious. Don't ruin the moment with insecurity and nerves.

"I'd have thought the kiss last night was a dead giveaway," he said.

Not only didn't he avoid it, he'd brought it right up! They were going to talk about it—and talking about it was good. "And the problem you mentioned?"

Because by that, and with my lighthearted expression and little lilt to my voice just then, I'm clearly telling you, there is no problem.

His hands were firmly on the stroller handles. "Our relationship has to be strictly professional, Molly. I'm your boss. There's a line I can't cross. Won't cross." He shook his head. "This is nuts. I shouldn't have said anything just now. Also unprofessional. I guess I'm thinking out loud and you're so truly my right hand that I clearly need your take on things too much. You're too indispensable."

She laughed. "Well, guess you can't fire me, then."

"No. Even if you were the worst administrative assistant in Wyoming I couldn't fire you *because* I kissed you. You'd be perfectly in your right to sue me for wrongful termination and sexual harassment, Molly. Boundaries are vital in the workplace, and I take them seriously."

"So the reason you won't kiss me again, the *only*

reason, is because you're my boss?" She held her breath and waited.

He stared at her for a second, his grip getting tighter on the stroller handles. He glanced away, looking up toward the path. "No. Not the only reason. For another, you're a parent, and you know my take on having a family of my own, so getting involved would be wrong."

"I thought you said the right woman could turn you around, change your mind," she countered, her stomach churning. She was going to lose in this back-and-forth.

"You're not the right woman, Molly. You can't be. Because you're my administrative assistant. End of story. Shall we go?" he added…tensely.

"In a second. I just want to understand. You kissed me last night because…?"

He let out a breath and looked down at the ground…well, Lucy's pink-hatted head. "A little crush, I guess. I like you, clearly we have a great rapport and you're lovely, Molly. I acted without thinking and I had no right."

She was swooning. *Lovely. Lovely. Lovely.*

"And for the reasons I stated," he added, "that kiss, our rapport, any of it, can't be explored further. But it's all right because I've already figured out a solution."

She almost puckered up. *Go ahead, kiss me passionately. If you're thinking that'll get me out of your system, you're so wrong, bucko.*

"I'm going to ask out Danica at our meeting tomorrow," he said, deflating the hope-balloon that had risen inside her. "I'll just focus on the plan—which has always been to win her heart. I'm sure when she says yes, thanks to your great tips and advice, my silly little crush on you will vanish. I mean, my feelings for Danica go way back."

Molly bit her lip, her heart sinking and falling over. *Glunk.*

Oh, now it's a silly little crush?

And his feelings for Danica were *real*? Um, had they not just gone over this last night in great detail?

Ah, he's trying, she realized. *Trying very hard to find a way out of his feelings for me. They're new and unsettling so he's rattled. He's just working out a plan to deal with it.* Suddenly, she didn't feel so bad. The man was turned inside out. Because of her!

"Anyway, I treasure you, Molly. After just one week you truly are indispensable to me. So strictly professional from here on in. And I'll go after my long-term crush and all this will be a distant memory we won't even remember to cringe about at the watercooler."

Humph. Not so fast. *If my ridiculous hair and bare face have you this attracted—to the point that you have to do something about it, like try not to be—imagine what spending more time with me will do?* And they had a few hours stretched out before them. Just him. Her. And her baby.

And come on—Molly liked her job a lot, but most of the reason was because of her boss. If being his admin would create problems for him, for them, and she understood his reasoning, there were plenty of other jobs out there. Then she'd only have the issue of his block about fatherhood to deal with, and she truly believed that Zeke Dawson was a born dad.

The man's hands were still on the stroller, and in fact, at the moment, he was making sure Lucy's buckles were secure and that her pink mittens were on her little hands securely.

Oh, Zeke.

With all *that* settled, Zeke sucked in a shallow breath and started pushing the stroller toward the path since he needed to do something.

Why had he actually confessed his feelings to her? What the hell was wrong with him?

Well, he knew what. His *feelings* for her in the first place. Like his brother had said this morning, Zeke had been kicked upside the head. He wasn't himself, not one bit. Zeke was usually a cool customer.

Oh, man. He had to get over this. His three or four hours with Molly at the ranch would help. He'd think of her *solely* as his admin, who he was showing around the property as promised. No worries. Her baby was with them, after all, and everyone, including him and Molly, knew he had no interest in being a father or a family man, so this was just a "winter outing" for the company, like his former employer used to hold every summer. Colleagues gathered at the beach or a park, families invited, cookouts and badminton. This was just like that. And it was just the three of them because he had a two-person office, dammit.

They headed up the path, Noah and Sara's "foreman" cabin coming into view and, beyond it up the hill, the majestic white farmhouse that he'd grown up in.

Molly stopped for a moment, shielding her eyes from the bright sun as she looked around. "When you told Lucy there's no more beautiful place than right here, you were absolutely right. And it's not just the natural beauty. It's everything. The history, the family legacy."

He appreciated the change in subject and felt his shoulders relax, a knot unwind. "Very true. I'm thinking about building a house on the land like Rex and Axel did. The property is huge. Axel's log mansion is five miles out and it's like he's in his own town, population three point five." But that suited Axel, since he led wilderness tours for the ranch and directed guest safety.

She grinned. "The point five for the baby to be?"

He nodded. "But I'm not sure what I want yet. House on the ranch? Or one in town, walking distance to the office? That would be nice. In all seasons. We'll see. Danica is one of the top Realtors in Bear Ridge. If there's a house meant for me in town, I'm sure she'll help me find it."

"She's great at her job," Molly said, then looked up ahead toward the path that veered to the right and the main buildings of the ranch. "I haven't been here in so long." She stared up at the farmhouse. "But I feel that old excitement. I used to run to the petting zoo, dying to see the black goats. They were my favorites. There were two."

"Barnaby and Beatrice. Their great-great-great-great-grandchildren are here now."

Molly's eyes widened. "Wow! But how is that possible? Wasn't the ranch shut down for several years?"

He nodded. "Within a few years of inheriting, my dad had sold most of the animals to pay for his drinking and gambling habits—not listening to reason that he was going to destroy the ranch and have nothing left. But when Noah decided to rebuild, he and Daisy bought many of the animals or their offspring back."

She seemed to take that all in. "That must have been so hard, watching your dad hurt himself and the ranch."

Zeke nodded, trying not to let his mind go back to some of those dark times.

"I think losing Leah—his third wife, Noah and Daisy's mother—just did him in," Zeke said. "His old fighting spirit went out of him." He shrugged. "I don't know. I don't claim to have known Bo Dawson very well. It's part of what makes me worry about myself as someone's husband, someone's father."

He could feel her looking at him and he glanced toward the barn that housed the petting zoo. Once again, he'd said too much because Molly Orton was too easy to talk to. He could tell her anything.

"I think I know what you mean. Because your

dad had his faults, but he also had his good points. It's not easy to classify someone. People are multifaceted. So maybe you figure that being a good guy like yourself doesn't mean you'll win any father of the year of awards. That maybe you, too, will be capable of hurting the people you love most."

He stopped in his tracks and turned to her, his hands clutching the stroller handles. "How do you do that? How do you always know what I mean when even I'm not sure?"

"Some people just get each other," she said. "You seem to get me, too."

He nodded and resumed walking. "That rapport I was talking about."

But it felt like much more than just rapport. He had *rapport* with a lot of people. This…chemistry between him and Molly was something else. Back before his sister fell in love with her husband, Daisy used to say she believed her soul mate was out there, and Zeke had dismissed the notion as airy-fairy. But everything that had summed up Daisy's idea of a soul mate was what he and Molly seemed to have.

Maybe this was what best friendship was. Zeke had had a few close friends over the years, though they'd drifted apart for moves and life shifts. His family had remained the people always there, the people he could count on, no matter what. It was true that Molly was beginning to feel like family.

Except for the fact that he was so attracted to her he could barely drag his eyes off her as they walked.

She's become your best friend in a very short period of time, he reminded himself. *Your indispensable best friend slash admin who runs your office and your schedule and you already can't do without her. Just focus on getting that first date with Danica and things will fall back to normal. Molly back into the friend zone. Danica into your love life.*

A loud bleat sounded and Molly laughed. "Hear that, Lucy? That sounds like a happy lamb to me."

"Ba la!" Lucy said, waving her arms.

"It's so great that the Dawson Family Guest Ranch has generations of Dawsons and generations of livestock," Molly said. "A true family affair all around."

He smiled. "It is pretty special," he said as they turned onto the path for the petting zoo. "Circle of life."

Molly's warm smile made him want to pull her into a hug and never let her go, but he kept his hands firmly on the stroller, except to raise one to wave at guests and some ranch employees as they headed toward the cafeteria.

Inside the barn, which was heated, they took off their coats, and Zeke almost did a double take at how sexy Molly looked in her off-white sweater and jeans. He did a slight head shake to clear it, telling himself to keep his eyes on her face.

They toured the petting zoo, which wasn't very crowded with guests since most seemed to be enjoying the warm-ish February day and were likely on horses or out hiking. They'd just gotten to the piglets when Lucy started yawning and by the lambs she was asleep.

"If you'd like her to have a proper nap," Zeke said, "I have a bassinet in my cabin, which is five seconds away from here. My sister-in-law Maisey used to live there before she and Rex got together, and they decided to leave some baby paraphernalia in the guest room for niece or nephew visitors. That's how Ford got to babysit just about every one of the little relatives whether he wanted to or not during the short time he lived there."

"He doesn't like kids?"

"Oh, he loves his nieces and nephews. But he's a little stiff around children. Talks to them like adults, that kind of thing. He's a detective, and he's always in cop mode, even at kiddie birthday parties."

She laughed. "Now I understand why he's the last holdout when it comes to getting married and having kids."

"And he *wants* kids. He's very ready to settle down. Ford will be a great dad, no doubt about it. He basically parented all his younger siblings."

Molly was studying him. "Huh. Interesting that you see the good father material in him but not yourself."

A lamb bleated again, so loud that Lucy stirred, her little face crumpling for a second. *Thank you, lamb, for that perfectly timed interruption.*

"I'd love to take you up on your offer of that bassinet," Molly said.

Now they'd be alone in his cabin. *Not the smartest move, Dawson.* How was he supposed to keep his thoughts platonic and professional when she looked so irresistibly sexy? All day he'd looked at her, into her brown eyes, and once or twice felt himself go weak in the knees.

Every time he thought he had a handle on his feelings for Molly, he found himself right back in the danger zone.

Chapter Eight

"This place is really cute," Molly said, looking around the small, cozy cabin that Zeke was calling home for now. There was a plush tan sofa and love seat, a huge sisal rug and a stone fireplace, plus two small bedrooms—one of which Lucy was sleeping peacefully in. She sat down on one end of the couch.

Zeke kneeled by the fireplace and put a log in and lit it, making the cabin even cozier. Romantic, she thought, staring into the flames. Of course, *that* obviously wasn't his intention, but still. "I've been staying here just a couple of days, but so far it's tipping the scales toward building on the ranch."

"Well, I can see why. The place is gorgeous and your family is here. You've got the river to the east and the mountains to the west, and all this wide open space."

He moved over to the wide front window, snow-covered evergreens in the distance. The cabin faced the ranch and seemed to be about a quarter mile from the lodge and cafeteria, but was set far back along the tree line that led to the mountains so that the immediate area was private. "Takes almost a half hour to get to town, though. I got used to walking to work in Cheyenne. I lived and worked downtown."

She wanted to know everything about his years in Cheyenne. "Do you miss it?"

He turned to face her but stayed by the window. Keeping his distance? Probably. "Nah. Which surprises me because I've lived there the past thirteen years and always thought it was home. But it wasn't. This is home."

"Bear Ridge is definitely home for me, but my house isn't. I mean, I live there, but it's not home. It's just the place I moved after the divorce. I couldn't stand the idea of living in the house I used to with my ex, so we sold that. Danica showed me a few houses but not a single one felt right. So I've been renting all this time. She's always sending me links to listings, but nothing that makes me want to see it."

Neither of them could figure that out. Why would she rather rent than buy? She was throwing away money, wasn't she?

He walked over to the club chair perpendicular to the sofa and sat down. Yup—definitely social distancing from her. "Sounds like something is missing—maybe what you envisioned living in your forever home would be like."

The all-too familiar lonely blues gripped her for a moment. Some mornings, especially when she came downstairs to make coffee before Lucy woke up, she'd feel empowered and all "your life is your own," and sometimes she felt so alone she could cry—and would. "You know, I think that's it. That makes complete sense. Plus, I'm the first person in my family to get divorced. No one makes me feel weird about it, but I still do. Took me so long to get married that I thought I'd be married till I was ninety-two."

"Maybe buying a house as a single mom makes you feel like you're signing up for that life forever," he said.

She thought about that for a few seconds, then

shrugged. "Maybe. I don't know. But I am a single mom and this is my life. I should be living for *now* not for some maybe future."

"At least you *know* you want to get remarried. You know what you want."

Hmm, she thought, trying not to study every nuance of his expression, which was actually very neutral. Maybe he was more ambivalent about marriage and family than dead set against it. Perhaps that was why he'd said it was possible that the right woman could turn him around. That definitely gave her more to work with.

"I want love and partnership," she said. "The universal stuff everyone needs."

"Even though it clearly doesn't mean it'll work out?"

"My motto is 'once burned, choose more wisely next time.' That's how I altered that saying."

He laughed. "You're smart, Molly Orton. But when it comes to women, I'm an idiot. I got so duped back in Cheyenne I don't even trust myself to choose wisely."

Her chest ached for the heartache he'd been through. She envisioned him walking through city streets, alone and hurting, so far from his family, from everything that could bring him instant comfort.

And something made a little more sense to her now. Something she'd been thinking about, wondering about. She wasn't sure she should say it, though.

"Out with it," he said, narrowing his eyes at her with a wary smile. "I can see those brown eyes working."

"Well, what you just said about not trusting yourself to choose wisely. I figure that might be why you're so focused on the old dream, the old crush. It lets you off the hook. Whether or not Danica is right for you isn't really the point. She's a placeholder."

All remnants of the smile were gone. "What?" he asked, staring at her.

Oh, boy. Talk about "personal nitty-gritty." *Well, you started it, Molly, so you might as well keep going and explain yourself.* "I think you're stuck right now, Zeke. And just when you needed something to jolt you, you heard Danica was single and that helped you decide to move back home so that you could finally have your shot at the woman of your dreams. Your focus is on the old because it's safe and probably not gonna happen, just like it never did before."

He did not look pleased with her analysis. At all.

"I don't agree," he said. "There's nothing safe

about uprooting your life. There's nothing safe about going for a dream, no matter how old."

She bit her lip, considering that. "That's very true. I just meant—"

"Maybe we should change the subject, Molly." He leaned back, glancing out the window. Then anywhere but at her.

She'd definitely struck a nerve.

"Want some coffee?" he asked, his expression anything but neutral now.

"Zeke, I'm sorry. I overstepped. We just start talking and, like you said, we can talk about anything and it gets very real very fast. So honesty just pours out of my mouth."

Except for the biggest truth of all. That I love you.

"Honesty is good," he said.

He could have called her out on her own holding pattern. Living in the rental when she had a down payment sitting in the bank. Waiting for her future instead of living her present. She hadn't realized she'd been doing that.

"I'll skip coffee. I'll wait for that cafeteria lunch you mentioned. I remember having the best chili of my life in the ranch caf. And great omelets and crispy bacon."

He brightened at the change of subject. "The

chef—Cowboy Joe—is the best. Everyone raves about his cooking. Did you know he married a guest? Ranch romances aren't that common. Well, except for the Dawsons. Noah got together with his wife, Sara, when she was hired as foreman—forewoman. Daisy met her husband when he was a guest. Axel's wife, Sadie, was also a guest here for a family reunion—it's her aunt who married Cowboy Joe. And Rex's wife, Maisey, is the head nanny at the ranch."

"Well, you and Danica would break the pattern, so that's a no go," she said on a chuckle, then mentally slapped her forehead for that one. She didn't need to put Danica in his head any more than she was already.

"True," he said with a smile. "I suppose if she helps me find a house in town, we'll be a town romance instead of a ranch romance."

"I don't see it," Molly blurted out, then clamped her mouth shut.

Oh, foo. She hadn't meant to say it, but dammit, she'd been thinking it.

He tilted his head. "What do you mean? Are you saying you don't see Danica and me as a couple? Is that why you were being kind of negative about me and her before?"

She bit her lip. "I don't know why I said that.

I take it back." He had to know she had feelings for him since she'd made it clear the kiss had been welcome. Maybe he was deliberately not going there since he'd decided they couldn't be and that he'd focus on his original crush: Danica.

"No, you said it for a reason."

Yes, because I see us together.

"Well, you two don't seem like peas in a pod," Molly finally said. "But that doesn't mean anything," she found herself adding because he did seem to value her opinion. "It's all about chemistry, right?"

"Exactly. So Danica and I aren't peas." He glanced out the window again and seemed to be thinking. "Maybe you should give me more intel. I've noticed her around town a couple times the past week—both times with a man. So she's definitely still dating. What is she looking for in a guy?"

"She's looking for what we're all looking for."

"What's that?"

"The right fit," Molly said. "Someone we connect with. Someone kind. Someone who feels like home. Someone who makes us smile. Inspires us to be our best self. Someone who has our back, pulls us up. Someone we can imagine sitting beside on the rocking chairs forty years from now."

He smiled. "I'm not sure I was looking that far ahead."

She tilted her head. "But you sound so serious about wanting to date Danica. Aren't you after a serious relationship with her?"

He glanced out the window again. "Maybe what you said before isn't so far off the mark, after all. That I'm stuck in some kind of holding pattern, unable to move at all, holding on to an old dream about a woman I've barely spoken to."

So she *had* struck a nerve.

"Well, all you can do is discover if the fantasy of Danica Dunbar meets the reality."

"Yeah," he said, brightening again. "That's a great way to put it. I'm sure it will. What's she like, anyway?" He frowned. "That sounds ridiculous, huh. Asking what my dream woman since eighth grade is like."

"She's as great as you imagine, Zeke," she said, picturing Danica coming over every night for a month after Molly's husband told her he was in love with his redheaded mechanic. Sitting up with her till all hours as Molly cried. Danica had always been there for her—with an ear, a shoulder, a smile. And had been for over twenty years.

Zeke beamed. "I knew it. But of course, you're biased—you two are best friends."

"For a reason. Because she is that wonderful. I remember when I first met her, in second grade, and we were paired as partners for a book report. I thought, *Oh, no, she's gonna be a stuck-up snot and make a snide comment on my weird multi-colored pants*. But she was friendly and kind and funny and we hit it off right away. We just have a similar something—I can't really put my finger on it."

"Now you're making me wish I had a best friend like that," he said. "I suppose I do in my siblings. But to be honest, Molly, you're the next closest thing."

Straight to the heart.

Except I'm your employee. And I have a baby...

She could fix the first, not that she wanted to. But Molly and Lucy were a pair, a team, a family. And yeah, the right woman could "turn him around," but Zeke didn't want to be attracted to her, didn't want to like her.

"I've never had a male best friend," she said. "Don't they—whoever *they* are—say men and women really can't be friends?" Molly figured men and woman could absolutely be friends. But maybe not when there was fire-hot chemistry between them.

"Well, *we* can be," he said. "Now that we've settled that whole kiss thing."

She gave a mental sigh. Hardly settled. And the cozy cabin that was supposed to have him barely able to control himself while in her presence had turned into friend-zone city. They were getting closer and closer as friends—and further and further as romantic possibilities.

Her strategy wasn't working at all. And now tomorrow he and her best friend could possibly become a couple, all thanks to good old Molly.

By ten o'clock that night, Molly was ready to pick her up phone and call Danica and tell her everything—that she was worried Danica and Zeke would fall madly in love tomorrow during their realty meeting and run off to Vegas for an instant wedding. Molly would finally share her secret—that she'd been in love with Zeke since seventh grade and was finally trying to make something happen between them…that something *had* happened until Zeke called a grinding halt to it.

She paused at her kitchen counter with one hand on the spray bottle of lemony cleaning solution and the other clutching a paper towel. Because she cared about Zeke so much, how could *she* put a grinding halt to anything happening between him and Danica? All she had to do was tell Danica how she felt about Zeke, and her BFF would friend-zone Zeke in a heartbeat—even if Danica wanted to go out with him.

Molly loved Zeke with everything she was. How could she manipulate things behind the scenes to serve *her* purposes?

She couldn't. And wouldn't.

They'd been so raw and honest with each other in his cabin. And true to his word, he remained at a physical distance while they'd been there, waiting for Lucy to wake up from her nap. No touching her hair. No putting his lips to hers. For a moment there, once or twice, she'd almost touched him herself—a simple hand to his forearm while making a point. But she had to respect what he'd said about the complications of his being her boss. An hour later, Lucy had woken up, and they'd gone to the ranch cafeteria, where they'd both had the incredible chicken chili and corn bread that had melted in her mouth. After lunch he'd showed her around the ranch, the guest cabins, which she well remembered, the river she'd tossed pebbles in. But then the weather took a cold turn and they skipped the hike and headed back, Zeke dropping off Molly and Lucy at her car by the Welcome hut.

A perfect day—and none of her goals accomplished. She'd gotten no closer to making Zeke hers than she'd been yesterday.

Molly finished cleaning the kitchen counter, then shut off all the lights and headed upstairs to her bedroom. She checked in on Lucy, who was fast asleep, her sweet baby girl reminding her that all was well and good in her life.

Molly left the nursery with one thing echoing in her head: if Zeke and Danica meet tomorrow and it was all parades and cartoon hearts and walking off into the sunset, then that was meant to be, and she and Zeke were not. Molly had always been a big believer in *meant to be*. It comforted her even if it hurt.

I'm going to lose him tomorrow. I'll be Danica's maid of honor at their wedding.

Molly frowned, her stomach flip-flopping, and picked up her phone. All she had to do was press the number two, the insta-speed-press for Danica's number, and just finally tell her the truth, that she loved Zeke, that it would kill her if Danica went out with him. That Zeke would be in her office tomorrow, and because he was so hot and nice and everything any woman would be looking for, Dancia would fall madly in love with him. And he with her.

Molly's finger hovered over the two button. She put the phone down, her heart hammering. She couldn't do that to Zeke. Or Danica. If those two belonged together, non-peas-in-a-pod aside, it would happen. Molly wouldn't interfere to save her own heart.

Her phone rang, startling her, and she practically jumped.

Danica.

Obviously, the universe *wanted* Molly to tell Danica her big secret.

Wait a minute. Molly had forgotten that Danica had her dog-walking date with the cute welder today. She'd been so wrapped up in herself she'd forgotten to check in with her friend. Given that Danica hadn't called or texted until now, maybe the two of them had had an extended date and they were the ones who'd be hitting the Vegas strip for the insta-wedding.

"Hi, Danica. How was your date with the welder?"

"Mol…ly," Danica sputtered between sobs. "He…big…liarrrr." Danica was crying and sniffling.

Oh, no. "Oh, honey. Are you home?"

"Yes," Danica managed on a sob.

"I'll be there in ten minutes."

"'K," Danica said tearfully.

Molly texted her dad to ask if he or her mom or both could watch Lucy for an hour or two, and her parents were over within minutes. Tomorrow was the grand reopening for Tim's Tasty Tacos, so her parents were wide awake and had come over with their iPads, deep in conversation about their cardboard take-out containers and if they should change colors. Molly thanked them again for coming, grabbed two pints of Ben & Jerry's from the freezer and rushed out to drive over to Danica's house, which was just five minutes away.

Unlike Molly, Danica had kept the house in her divorce, since she'd chosen it and decorated it and loved it. Brick with a fairy-tale cottage vibe, the house had been Molly's home away from home for years. Danica had gotten rid of anything that reminded her of her marriage and redid the place so that it was now like a beach cottage getaway. Molly loved it.

Danica came to the door in her hot-pink fluffy bathrobe, her hair in a ponytail, her eyes red-rimmed, her face tear-streaked. She threw her arms around Molly. "I'm never dating again. That's it. I give up."

"Aww, I'm so sorry," Molly said, slinging her free arm around her friend's shoulder. "Let's go dish these up," she added, holding up the two pints of ice cream. "We'll mix 'em." Mixing was their tradition.

Danica nodded and sniffled and led the way to the kitchen. "I'm *never* dating again," she repeated, throwing her hands up.

"Tell me everything," Molly said, scooping out one pint while Danica did the other. With their bowls full of a scrumptious mix of chocolate-fudge-caramel-marshmallow and coffee-espresso-chip, they headed to the couch.

Danica flopped down and ate a bite. "Ahhh, so good. Okay, here goes the whole sorry story." She took another spoonful of ice cream, then dabbed under her eyes. Molly was glad to see sparks of anger taking over the tears. "We met in the park and he seemed wonderful. Off we go with his adorable dog, Petey, who he tells me about rescuing from a crowded shelter all the way in Texas, where he used to live, and how he's a former marine who did two tours in Afghanistan, and how now he volunteers twice a week with a program for boys who don't have father figures."

Hmm, did the welder sound a little too good to be true?

"I'm thinking he's just amazing," Danica continued. "I thought—finally—I *feel* something. Excitement and possibilities. We have such a great time. He asks me if I'd like to continue the date with dinner—at Matteo's—that new pricey romantic Italian restaurant. So we both go home, and I prep for this date in all my glory. I get to the restaurant and he's charming and wonderful, asking all about me, listening intently. Doesn't cross a single Molly Orton line!"

Molly offered a smile. "I can see why you were excited about him."

Danica ate two more spoonfuls of ice cream. "The bill comes and he reaches for his wallet and then gets all flustered and says, 'I'm so embarrassed—I forgot my wallet.' So I think nothing of it and say, 'There's no reason why you should pay for dinner just because you're a man.' He profusely apologizes and says he'll more than make it up to me tomorrow night, if I'd be willing to see him again, in Prairie City for the new sushi bar that opened. Then a woman comes marching up to our table and demands to know who I am and she thought 'Declan' was visiting his sick mother. He told me his name was Jack! Oh, and turns out he's married. And the dog? His neighbor's."

Molly shook her head. "Oh, foo, I'm so sorry." After the last few dud dates Danica had, no wonder she felt so defeated by this con man.

The angry spark in her pretty blue eyes was

once again replaced by tears welling. "He had me believing every word out of his lying mouth. I fell for everything. How can I trust anything anyone says again?"

"There are good guys out there," Molly said, reaching for her friend's hand and giving it a gentle squeeze. "You're playing a numbers game because you know you have to kiss frogs to find your Mr. Right. Tonight was a poisonous toad. One poisonous toad. Don't let this jerk derail your faith in the good men out there."

Danica seemed to consider that. "You're right. And at least he didn't con me out of more than just a dinner." She sighed. "I think I'll take a break from dating, though. Just for a little while. Unless the greatest guy on earth falls into my lap and passes every one of your tests."

Uh-oh. Tomorrow, that guy would be Zeke.

Molly shoveled another spoonful of ice cream in her mouth, barely tasting it.

"Thanks for coming over," Danica said. "I feel a lot better."

Molly hugged her friend. "Want to do seaweed face masks before I go?" Danica's green face mask did for her friend what potato chips and onion dip did for Molly.

Danica laughed. "Of course I do. No more crying over frogs."

Molly grinned and they headed off to the bathroom, where Danica's tear-streaked face and red-rimmed eyes would be a thing of the past for her meeting tomorrow with a prince.

Chapter Nine

Zeke had gone to sleep last night thinking about Molly. He woke up thinking about her.

He'd spent too much of his morning at work thinking about her.

When he'd arrived at 8:40, figuring he'd get to work first and could slip into his office without being overwhelmed by his attraction to her, there she was. Sitting at her desk, typing away on her desktop computer, Dawson Solutions coffee mug in front of her. Her hair had been in a bun, and he'd wanted to release the clip holding it. He'd wanted to undo the little leaf-patterned scarf at her neck. Slip her suit jacket off her shoulders…

It was now close to noon; he'd gotten little accomplished, and he was ready to go get his brain back to normal, back on track, by meeting with Danica Dunbar at Bear Ridge Realty. Surely once he was enveloped in the midst of his dream woman, he would refocus and his crush—if that was what it was—on his admin would disappear.

He came down the hall toward the reception area, and Molly stopped typing. "Well, wish me luck."

"You won't need it," she said. "I'd straighten your tie knot like in the movies but your tie is perfect."

He smiled. "See you this afternoon. I'll tell you all about it."

The office phone rang and she grabbed it, so that was that. Time to go.

Outside, he breathed in the cold but fresh, crisp air and headed left. Blue Ridge Realty was three doors down. There were some glossy photos in the window of homes for sale—from huge ranches to small houses in town.

Here goes fifteen years of waiting, he thought, pulling open the door. Danica came right over, extending her hand.

"Zeke, so nice to see you again," she said.

Just as when he saw her last week for the first time since high school, he waited for the rush of emotion—excitement, anticipation—but all he felt was interest in finding out more about available houses in Bear Ridge.

Very weird. This was Danica Dunbar, standing before him wearing a pink-and-white tweed minisuit and very high heels, her long blond hair in a low ponytail curled down one shoulder. Makeup, jewelry—all business-glam. She looked amazing and did smell heavenly. But the face that had starred in his dreams all these years, that had gotten him through some very trying times, didn't seem to be affecting him. In the slightest. Not even in a nostalgic way.

How would he stop thinking about Molly if he wasn't consumed by his crush?

She led him to her desk. A credenza with a lot of vases of flowers was against the wall. From her suitors, he figured. No red tulips, Danica's favorite, per Molly. A few days ago he would have ordered an exquisite arrangement of three dozen to be delivered after a meeting like this. Now, everything was up in the air.

"So," she said, sitting down in her swivel chair and gesturing for him to sit in the leather club chair across. She held an iPad and a stylus pen. "You gave me a brief rundown of what you're looking for when you called the other day, but I'd like to hear more detail about what's important to you in a house. Location. Square footage. Number of bedrooms and bathrooms. Style. Privacy. We'll start there and see what's available."

He looked right at her, wondering what the hell was wrong with him. Shouldn't he be unable to think, let alone concentrate on all she'd just said? Shouldn't he be unable to drag his eyes off her pretty blue eyes, the shimmery pink-red lipstick, her long legs?

His head was actually full of house details. He kept thinking about the luxe cabins—Daisy called them log mansions—that his brothers Axel and Zeke had built on the ranch property. He could see himself in something like that. Or the classic farmhouse Ford had bought in town. He liked that, too. He kept waiting to be distracted from his thoughts by Danica's beauty, but right now all he thought about was a section of the ranch down by the river, three miles from where the path along the water ended—where the guests turned around on their walks. That area would be perfect and private. And right there on the ranch with his family.

"Full disclosure," he said. "I might very well

decide to build on my family's property, but I'm not sure of that. I do like the idea of walking to work, though. I also like space and large rooms. I'm not really sure about number of bedrooms. To be honest, I don't know what I want."

I thought I wanted you.

I thought I'd never have kids of my own—and now I can't stop thinking about a single mother with a year-old baby who likes to grab my ear.

"Well, right now you're single," Danica said. "But if you're planning to marry and start a family, that may be something to consider when it comes to space. The new condos that went up on the far side of Main Street are beautiful, but they're one- and two-bedroom. A condo might serve a 'right for now' purpose."

"That *would* let me off the hook," he mused aloud.

"What do you mean?"

Part of him was vaguely aware that he should shut up. But he kept going. "Just that I never planned to marry or have kids at all. But then you meet someone, and bam, your whole point of view is different."

Am I talking about Molly? Or Danica?

She nodded. "I'm glad to hear that because I'm not sure *I* want kids. Maybe I just haven't been hit with baby fever yet. But I do think my Mr. Right, if he wants children, will fire up those maternal instincts." She shrugged. "I don't know. My ex-husband didn't, which is why he divorced me." She bit her lip. "Oh, God, did I just say that aloud? Do you know I haven't talked about this with anyone and here I am, just blurting it out?" She looked stricken. "Okay, back to houses. Condos. Square footage."

He stared at her, focusing on not allowing his mouth to drop wide open. She wasn't sure she wanted children. She was him in male form!

So why wasn't this having a bigger impact? He could ask her out right now, mentioning that he'd love to talk more about this complex topic over dinner at her favorite restaurant in Prairie City.

But he couldn't even summon the interest in asking her out. When she was even more perfect for him than he knew ten minutes ago.

"I guess the most important thing is keeping an open mind—and staying true to yourself," she said. "So what do you think? Want to look at houses and the condos? I know of four within walking distance to Main Street that may fit the bill—they're all a little different. Two have turn-of-the-last-century charm and two are recent builds."

"I'd like to see them all," he said. "It'll help me

decide to get a sense what's out there. I hope I'm not wasting your time. I'll understand if you'd prefer if we made an appointment for when I know what I want."

"All part of my job," she said with a warm smile.

They stood and headed toward the door. She opened the closet, handed him his overcoat and slipped on that long red wool coat with the leather belt she'd been wearing the first day he'd seen her. The day he'd met Molly. Re-met Molly. She tossed her long curled ponytail over down past one shoulder, a faint hint of her perfume in the air.

Still, absolutely nothing. Amazing. He wouldn't have thought it even possible.

As they got into her silver car, Danica added, "Sometimes you have to see that what you thought you wanted doesn't meet any of your needs. And sometimes, something you never would have put on the list is perfect. It can be a numbers game. And other times, you get lucky right off the bat and find your dream home with the first showing."

He stared at her, wondering if she knew about his old crush. Or that he'd kissed Molly and put the kibosh on that. After all, she and Molly were best friends, but they both clearly kept some truths to themselves. From Danica's expression and voice, with absolutely zero personal glint in her eyes, he decided she was just speaking generally. A little too applicable, though.

"So we have something big in common besides Bear Ridge High class of too many years ago," she said as she headed into the light traffic.

He glanced at her. "What's that?"

"Molly! Isn't she just the best?"

She sure is, he thought. "I'm lucky to have her as my administrative assistant. Do you happen to know what her favorite flowers are? She did a great job on client research this morning, and I'd like to thank her."

Danica beamed. "She loves red daisies. She calls them 'the day brightener.' If it were summer she'd pick them right out of her yard and have a bunch on her desk."

"Perfect," he said. "Thanks."

She smiled, and he couldn't help but think about how he used to wish she'd turn that beautiful smile on him in the halls at school, on Main Street as teens. But now, Danica Dunbar was simply a lovely human being and highly recommended Realtor who was showing him houses. And that she knew Molly's favorite flowers was quite a plus.

Why did it seem everything was reversed now?

Maybe they should look at the one-bedroom

condos first—and he should buy one. No room for the family he was sure he didn't want.

"So which would you like to see first? The houses or the condos?"

Say condos. Say condos.

"The houses," he found himself saying.

Molly had barely eaten three bites of the turkey-and-cheese sandwich she'd packed for today's lunch. Were Danica and Zeke making out right now on some scenic overlook? In an empty house she was showing him? Had he already asked Danica out for every night of the rest of their lives?

She forced herself not to bite her nails. She'd been so consumed with thoughts about the date she'd almost forgotten today was the grand turnaround of Tim's Tasty Tacos. She'd called her dad just a little while ago and the moment he'd answered the phone she knew business was booming.

She glanced out the front window of Dawson Solutions only to see Zeke coming across Main Street with a bouquet of red daisies. Her favorite flowers. Sigh. He must have forgotten that Danica's favorite flowers were red *tulips*, which wasn't like him. Her boss remembered everything. Her friend liked all flowers, but for a man gunning to win

Danica's heart, daisies didn't seem very "grand gesture."

She expected him to turn left toward Bear Ridge Realty, but he came into Dawson Solutions. "Afternoon, Molly. I miss anything?"

Forget what you *missed—what did* I *miss?*

She sat up straight and reminded herself she was at work. "Several calls from potential clients interested in meetings, a call from Peter Winkowski and a request for a follow-up meeting from Shelly Neffer."

He nodded and held out the bouquet. "For you. For all your hard work on the Ranelli account. Your research was impeccable and saved me countless hours."

Molly tilted her head. "These are for me?"

"They are. I got a tip that red daisies are your favorite."

Her heart gave a little ping. "Well, thank you, Zeke." She popped up to get a vase from a cabinet at the coffee station, filled it with water and put in the pretty bouquet. Zeke Dawson had given her flowers! For a moment, everything else went out of her head.

But as she set them on her desk, her burning question came right back and she couldn't wait a second longer. "So was the meeting…successful?" *Did you ask her out?*

"Danica showed me two condos and three houses, but none of them was quite right for different reasons. I'm going to take one of the buggies out on the ranch this weekend to explore some areas and think more about building on the property."

She nodded slowly, waiting for him to keep going, to mention that he finally had gotten his date with Danica and they were going out Saturday night.

"At first I thought a high-end one-bedroom condo would suit me fine," he said, "but what if I wanted to have my nieces and nephews over? They'd crash into each other in such a small place. Danica pointed that out."

Molly kept waiting for him to get around to his finally asking Danica out after years of waiting. But he was talking houses and how the small yards wouldn't work if his siblings with dogs wanted to come for a barbecue.

"What's the point of a yard if I can't throw sticks for Dude and River?" he said. "Fetch is one of their favorite things. And my nephew Danny? Two years old and already headed for captain of the track team. I'd probably want to build a play-house for all of them, too."

Sounded like a man who was in the beginning stages of thinking ahead to a family of his own. A dog of his own.

Because Danica would turn him around.

A lump formed in Molly's throat.

"So when's the big date?" she asked. "Saturday night?"

Zeke looked at her as if she'd grown another nose. "Date? Well, that hardly seems really appropriate since she's my Realtor now. Don't you think?"

Molly gave a dry chuckle. Ha, ha, real funny. He was making fun of *their* situation, wasn't he? Which didn't seem like him, but perhaps he needed to make light of it. Sweep it all under the ole rug.

But not only wasn't he laughing, he wasn't smiling. "I'm serious."

"Wait, what?" she asked. "You are?"

"It's a working relationship. Realtor and client. I think business and romance should be kept separate. And not just in a boss and subordinate situation but in all cases. I told you I got burned with a former colleague, so that's probably just too fresh. Maybe once I'm settled on a house—either in town or on the ranch—I'll revisit asking her out. If she's not seriously involved with someone by then."

Molly forced her jaw not to drop to her lap. What in the world? Okay, yes, he had been hurt by a former coworker. But c'mon. His Realtor was *not* his colleague. He was making excuses for not asking out Danica Dunbar, woman of his dreams. If Zeke had asked Danica out, she likely would have said yes.

Because she had no idea that Molly was madly in love with the man.

So what gives?

As Zeke stood in front of her desk flipping through the messages she'd taken, she studied him. Carefully. He looked so…content. At peace.

Wait. A. Minute. Another possibility occurred to her. Could it be? Was it actually possible?

Had Zeke discovered that he didn't actually *have* a crush on Danica anymore?

"Zeke, I'd like to ask you a personal question. You don't have to answer, of course."

"Okay," he said. Warily.

"You spent almost three hours with Danica this afternoon. Was it like you expected—I mean, on a personal level?"

She was getting the clear sense it *wasn't*. Or he would have asked Danica out instead of coming up with a flimsy excuse about business and pleasure. She wanted to stand up on her chair and do a little happy dance.

"It was," he said very seriously.

Her heart thumped and she stared at him. "Oh." Had he been too choked up with emotion to ask Danica out? Had he gotten tongue-tied from being so close to her?

"I've known for a few days now that the old crush is gone," he continued. "But I was hoping it would still be there so I could distract myself." He paled for a moment as if he hadn't meant to say that last part.

Oh! Her frown was immediately turned upside down. The twenty-year crush on Danica Dunbar was over. Because he had feelings for Molly! She glanced at her vase of sweet red daisies, her heart leaping around in her chest.

"Well, I'd better get to work," he said. "I took a long few hours to myself, so…"

"Of course," she said in her professional voice, scooting her chair in and poising her hands over her keyboard. She fought the grin bursting inside her as he headed down the hall toward his office— very possibly thinking about *her*.

There was still the matter of his certainty that he doesn't want to be a father, she realized. She bit her lip. He'd said that outright a number of times and it came from somewhere deep inside him, as rooted as his family tree.

But that was an old hanger-on—she was sure of it—just like his crush on Danica had been. Everything about Zeke—from his actions, behavior, conversation—centered on family and how important it was. So she'd just have to show the baby whisperer of Bear Ridge that he was made for fatherhood, made for a family of his own. That would take a blowtorch, though, to get through the cinder-block walls he'd erected around his heart.

But right now, Molly Orton felt like she could truly do *anything*.

Chapter Ten

"It's no use," Ford said, swiping the metal detector over a patch of ground between two trees. "I'm never going to find the diary."

"You'll find it," Zeke said, though he also had his doubts. They just had to keep looking.

The two of them were across from the barns at the ranch, wearing lighted helmets so they could see two inches in front of them in the dark. It was just past seven p.m., and this wasn't an optimal time to be looking for something outside. But Ford had texted him for help just as he'd been about to leave the office, and given Zeke's day, he needed to be in cold air, a constant shock to the system, doing something that would require concentration. Only way to stop thinking about Molly—especially now that he'd acknowledged, even to her, that his twenty-year crush on her friend was over.

It had been more than a year that Ford had been trying to find his late mother's diary, which their dad had buried in a metal box on the property decades ago. Ford would not even have known about it, but Bo Dawson had left Ford a map in his deathbed letter, detailing where he'd buried it. The map was in marker, with a lot of goofy-looking trees, dotted lines, something resembling the big barn and an *X* marks the spot. Apparently, Bo had found his then wife's diary and had been so incensed by whatever Ellen Dawson had said that he'd run out of the house with it in an old fishing tackle box, dug a hole, dropped it in and covered it back up. After reading the letter from his dad and looking at the map that Bo had drawn on a piece of white paper, Ford had tracked down an old friend of his mother's to ask if she knew what could have been in the diary that would have set off his dad. The friend said she had no idea but recalled Ellen had tried in vain to find it for weeks before storming out in a huff with her bags, taking Ford with her.

All the siblings wanted to know what was in that diary.

"Dad was clearly drunk when he drew the map," Zeke said as Ford swiped the metal detector again. "Maybe he buried it miles from here."

"Could be. But he drew this spot between the trees, straight down from the barns. I feel like it's probably here somewhere since there was no other reason to pick this area over another. Nothing special about it otherwise."

"It *is* close to the barns, though. Would he have buried the diary where someone could have easily seen him?"

"I thought about that. According to the story I heard secondhand from my mom's friend, it was the middle of the night when he buried it so no one except the night hands would have been around." He shrugged. "I should give up but I can't. I just feel like I'll find some missing piece of the story—my parents' story. My story." Ford's mother had died back when he was in the police academy, and Zeke recalled how grief-stricken his brother had been, vowing to push ahead with his training because his mother had been so proud that her only child was going to serve and protect.

"Well, let's keep looking," Zeke said. The past

few days had been on the warm side and the snow was mostly gone, making it easier.

"What was in your letter from Dad again?" Ford asked, squinting at Zeke. He could tell Ford was trying to remember.

"No maps, thankfully. He asked me to use my business sense to help Noah with the financials when he took on rebuilding the ranch."

Ford shook his head. "Now why couldn't Dad leave me a nice, uncomplicated letter like that? No, I get a map to buried anxiety."

Zeke smiled. "Maybe it's something good that set him off. I can't imagine what, though."

"Me, either. Oh, who the hell knows. I'm giving up for the day. For the week, I should say."

Ford limited himself to looking only one day a week. It's how he kept his sanity about the diary.

At first Zeke was bothered by his own letter from his father, that it contained nothing more than Bo's surprise at having a numbers whiz for a son and the request to help Noah. But once he'd started going over paperwork with Noah when the ranch was still a scrap heap, he realized what an undertaking his father had left him. Bo had no money to get the ranch going, and back then neither had Noah, but they'd all pooled their resources, Noah heading the job, hiring the crews, attending the livestock auctions, et cetera, and from afar and by video calls, Zeke had talked him through the books. Through it all, Zeke had felt he was rebuilding the ranch last spring with Noah and then Daisy, who'd come home to help. Maybe his dad hadn't thought beyond, *Well, you're a business guy and this is a business, so would you help?* Or maybe he thought a lot about it. All Zeke knew for sure was that he'd gotten closer to his family because of it. And *that* was priceless.

Zeke had stopped second-guessing Bo Dawson a long time ago. But the not knowing bugged him. When it came to his father, he could use a crystal ball that would provide answers. Zeke did not have an addictive personality, wasn't much of a drinker and wouldn't gamble even on buying a lottery ticket. But what if he *was* like Bo when it came to being a parent? What if, like his own father, Zeke wouldn't be there for his kids emotionally? What if he just checked out? How would he ever forgive himself? Lord knows he'd never forgiven his dad.

Work, work, work, his first girlfriend in Cheyenne had complained, eventually ending their relationship. He hadn't realized he was being a workaholic or keeping that ex on the outside. It was the *not* realizing, the having no clue he was hurting someone else, that kept him up at night.

Which was why he was trying so hard to let Molly know, from the get-go, that they couldn't explore what was clearly between them. The thought of hurting her—now that really kept him awake and popping Tums.

Zeke stared up at the twinkling stars, wishing he could blink his eyes and make himself sure he wouldn't let down those he cared about. He supposed he could talk to Ford about it again, but how many times was he going to ask the same question? He was getting the idea that the answers weren't going to come from outside himself.

A low honk sounded, and he and Ford both turned around.

It was Noah in one of the ranch carts. "Hey, Zeke, I'm on my rounds and you're just the brother I needed to talk to. On Saturday, I'm holding the inaugural Teen Rancher's Summit in the lodge. I thought I had the first day mapped out but I could use one more speaker and it's your area, if you're willing."

For a minute, Zeke had no idea what Noah was talking about, then remembered him bringing up the new initiative he'd started for the teens who attended the town's community center after school and on weekends. The center catered to low-income families and at-risk teenagers, and Noah, who'd been through the wringer as a teen and had some skirmishes with the law, had started a program meant to interest them in ranching and to inspire them in general. The posters he'd hung at the center had generated strong interest.

"What do you have in mind?" Zeke asked.

"A basic talk on money and how it works. How to get some if you have none—in a way that will make you proud instead of land you in jail. My talk will focus on how I started as a ranch hand with nothing. So how to save, have a goal and work toward it instead of blowing all your money on stuff that won't last. And some general encouragement on being successful and how that's individual to each. That kind of thing."

"Count me in," Zeke said. He was more than willing to help out. When he was a teen, he had a few great teachers who'd been encouraging and inspiring, and his siblings had been, too.

Noah pumped his fist in the air. "Great. I'll text you the details. I owe ya." He eyed Ford. "I'll be hitting you up in a couple weeks to talk about how to become a law enforcement officer. No one escapes my sibling resources."

Ford grinned. "Count me in, too. And in payment, next week you can help me look for the diary."

"Will do," Noah said. "Gotta get back to the cabin. I'm on twin duty tonight while Sara has a girls' night." He waved and drove off in the green cart.

Ford shook his head. "'As I live and breathe,' as my mom used to say. I'll never get used to the changes in Noah. Man, did he do a one-eighty. For a while there, I thought I'd end up arresting him one day. I used to think that about Dad. That one day I'd have to arrest my own father if I joined the Bear Ridge PD."

Zeke sucked in a breath. "Is that why you left in the first place?"

"Probably," Ford said.

And now Ford was ready to settle down, get married, have kids. Just like that. Why couldn't Zeke feel that way?

"Hey, Ford. This epiphany or whatever it is about being ready to get married and be a dad. Did it just come over you one day out of the blue or was it gradual?"

"You know what they say—gradual and then all of a sudden. I'm ready. Now I just have to find her."

Molly's pretty face floated into Zeke's mind,

her riotous curls bouncing around, brown eyes full of light and curiosity and passion for life. "What if it happened in reverse? If you maybe found the right woman but you weren't ready for all that forever stuff."

"Way I see it, if you recognize that someone is the right woman, you're ready."

Zeke almost jumped out of his skin. Just because he couldn't stop thinking of Molly, just because he lit up like a Christmas tree whenever he was with her, just because he found her baby girl precious, didn't mean she was the right woman.

And what made it even harder was that he couldn't separate Molly the admin from Molly the woman. He was entranced by the *complete* Molly Orton. But even if he wasn't her boss, he wouldn't be ready for a family. No, sir. Not by a long shot.

Ping.

A text from Molly.

Help! My parents are arguing like crazy. They need you—if you're available. I'm at their house.

Arguing already? That was a surprise. Tim's Tasty Tacos, with their new menu and location, had been a smash success since hour one of reopening this morning. Zeke hadn't had a chance to check out the truck for himself, but Tim had messaged him photos of the line of people waiting to order, regardless of the cold. Tim had also sent a selfie of him and his wife with their heads poked out the window, huge smiles on their faces.

So what had happened?

Be there in a half hour, he texted back. Tell them to stop arguing till I get there to mediate. That should help calm them down.

Thank you! You're the best.

No, Molly, you are.

When Zeke arrived at the Orton home, he could hear Tim and Abby arguing from their porch— with the door closed. What could possibly have happened? He'd been trying to speculate on the drive over but nothing made sense.

When Molly opened the door, she shook her head, the bickering all the louder.

"My father wants to sell Tim's Tasty Tacos," she whispered.

Zeke stared at her. "What?"

She shook her head again, worry and exasperation etched on her face.

Why on earth would Tim want to sell after all

he'd been through to turn the business around? Tim's Tasty Tacos was now a success.

He'd get to the bottom of it. "It'll be okay," he assured her. "Let's go talk to your dad."

The worry on her face had him wishing he could pull her into a hug, a quick one.

Which made him realize that he wanted to hug her because he *cared* about her. Deeply.

"We've had a great day of sales!" Abby Orton was saying as Zeke entered the kitchen with Molly. "People were lined up for our tacos from opening at eleven in the morning until we closed at six. And you want to *sell*? I don't understand!"

Tim, leaning against the counter holding a mug of coffee, lifted his chin. "I keep trying to explain my way of thinking to you, Abby, but you're not hearing me. I simply want to quit while we're ahead." He turned to Zeke. "Well, I don't know that Molly had to call you. I can take things from here."

"I think it's important for Zeke to be here," Molly said. "Just in case you and Mom need an impartial voice, Dad."

"Thank you for coming, Zeke," Abby said. She sat at the table, turning her own cup of coffee around and around. "I know it's late and I'd appreciate your take on things. Would you like some coffee? Tim just made a fresh pot."

"I'd love some," Zeke said. He knew to wait for information, not to press or push. The heart of the matter always came out faster, easier and more transparently that way.

Molly opened a cabinet and got out a mug. "I'll get it."

Zeke sent her a sympathetic smile. "Thanks, Molly."

Abby was staring at her husband. "So Mac Parker offers you a small fortune today for your brand-new successful business, and that's it. You're ready to hand it over just like that? I don't get it no matter how times you try to explain yourself!"

I don't, either, Molly mouthed to Zeke.

"We can recoup our money and take a trip, Abby," Tim said, his voice gentle. "You always wanted to see the red rocks of Utah."

Abby sighed. They'd clearly been having this same conversation. "Yes, *someday*. But what I want now is to work in Tim's Tasty Tacos! I had no idea how much I'd enjoy my second career. We've just started."

Tim took a sip of his coffee. "Well, I want to sell. I should be at the mini golf course and catching up on my reading, not working this hard."

Zeke studied Tim Orton's voice and body language, trying to hear what he wasn't saying, to read between the lines. But some vital information was missing here. Zeke knew it was coming, so he held tight and waited.

"And my stake in the business is fifty-one percent," Tim added, his voice a bit wobbly as if it had pained him to say those words. "You're the one who insisted on that, Abby, so that means I should decide."

Abby's face crumpled. "Because this was—*is*—your baby! Equal partners but with a smidge more to you since it was all your idea and your dream. And now you want to end it? I don't understand at all!" Abby threw her hands up, stood and dabbed under her eyes, then fled the room.

Molly stirred in one sugar and a dollop of cream and handed the mug of coffee to Zeke. He mouthed, *Thanks*, to her. Then she walked over to her father and put her hand on his arm. "Dad, I'm gonna go calm Mom down." She kissed her father on the cheek, sent Zeke a pleading look, then left the kitchen.

Once Molly's feet could be heard on the stairs, Tim turned to Zeke.

"I thought I wanted a taco truck, but I don't,"

Tim said. "It's a lot. And I can get a lot for it. I've changed my mind and that's that."

Zeke still wasn't sure what was going on with Tim. He needed to ask some pointed questions. "Tell me what went through your mind when the man your wife mentioned—Mac Parker?—offered to buy the business."

"Well, I was on my break at an off-peak time and window-shopping near the truck when Mac Parker came up to me. He asked me some questions about how business was going, said he saw the big lines today, and okay, I did brag a little about how well we're doing now. He made me an offer on the spot. A really good offer. Like I said, Abby and I would recoup the money we laid out and then some. We could finally go on that cruise we've been talking about, too."

Zeke took a sip of his coffee. "Who's Mac Parker?"

"Oh, we went to high school together. He was a real star back then. Captain of this and that. I was more the science fair type." He leaned closer. "I'll tell you, it sure felt good having Mac Parker want something of mine."

Ah. The crux of the matter.

"Of course, I didn't tell him what hard work it was," Tim added on a chuckle. "How much blood, sweat and tears go into creating one single taco. And heart, too—I mean, you've got to put your whole heart into it or the tacos will taste terrible. People know when there's real care, real feeling, involved. And not just in the tacos but every aspect of the business."

"I absolutely agree. And this Mac Parker—is he the type to put his heart into what he does?"

"Oh, please," Tim said, narrowing his eyes. "He's a silver platter type. Never had to work hard for anything. Opposite of me. And he's not exactly a nice person. I'll tell ya—I'll never forget how, senior year, I finally worked up the courage to join the cross-country team when he was captain, and I always came in second to last—every race. He used to rib me all the time. 'Hey, Orton, at least you're not as slow as the kid in the wheelchair.' God, what a jerk."

"So your business will go from Tim's Tasty Tacos to *Mac's* Tasty Tacos with no heart—or soul apparently."

"Yeah." He rolled his eyes. "Good luck with that, Mac."

Zeke took another sip of his coffee. He was getting closer. "And you want to sell to him now, when you're just starting, when business is booming your first day out, because…"

Tim frowned. "Because he wants it—and for a small fortune. I'm a success. Me, Tim Orton, middle manager in the Converse County Hospital IT department for thirty years. Sure, the truck is a hit now—it's a novelty, fun, easy menu. But if we kept it, eventually people will get bored and the lines will stop forming and the truck will fail and then guess who's not going to see the red rocks of Utah? Who will be left with nothing?" He turned away, looking out the kitchen window.

And there it was. The true heart of the matter: Fear of failure. Waiting for the ole other shoe to drop. For it all to be taken away—leaving not him but his wife with nothing. And Molly and Lucy without that rainy-day fund he'd talked about.

"Tim, I'm not big on risk. It's never been my game or strategy. I grew up with risk shadowing every corner of my life. I appreciate stability. Logic. A smart path forward. And with everything I know about business, my experience and instincts both tell me Tim's Tasty Tacos is going to be a fixture in Prairie City for as long as the business makes you happy."

Tim tilted his head. "Makes me happy? But I can't control how the business does. That can depend on so many factors."

"And the biggest factor is *you*. You and Abby.

Tim's Tasty Tacos is a success because you wanted this, you made it happen, you asked for help when it wasn't going the way you envisioned and you implemented changes that turned business around. You also smartly brought in your wife as your partner. You're a success because of you. It's not about taking risks or possibly failing. You're a success, Tim. All you have to do is keep doing what you're doing and tweak when necessary."

Tears welled in Tim's eyes. "I hate Mac Parker. That rat bastard. He can go to hell! And he's not taking my family business with him."

Zeke grinned. "Now you're talking."

"I've got loads of ideas if business ever stalls. So does Abby. We're gonna be just fine."

Zeke nodded. "Yes, you will. And if you ever need guidance, I'm a text away. You saw that tonight." He extended his hand.

Tim pulled him into a bear hug. "Thank you, Zeke. Once again, you've set me straight and saved my hide. I insist on paying you." He reached for his wallet.

Zeke held up a palm. "And I insist you don't. Molly called me in tonight. And she's a godsend."

Tim eyed him. "She sure is. Pretty, too."

Zeke's throat suddenly felt tight. "Very pretty."

Tim smiled, his eyes now bright and happy.

"Well, if you're not going to accept good old cash, I must insist you take this." He opened a cabinet and pulled out a bottle of tequila, orange liqueur and a small container of lime juice. He put everything in a red gift bag.

Footsteps sounded on the stairs. Molly came into the kitchen and eyed them both. "Dad, you look a lot happier than you did fifteen minutes ago."

"Everything's okay now, honey. I'm not selling the truck. Zeke here helped me understand a few things. Everything needs a Zeke."

Molly grinned and looked from her dad to Zeke, the warmth in her beautiful brown eyes making him almost blush. "Mom's going to be very happy."

"And this is for you two," Tim said, holding up the red bag. "All the mixings for classic margaritas— the perfect way to celebrate that Tim's Tasty Tacos is here to stay." He gave the bag to Molly with a big smile. "I'll go tell your mom the good news," he added before dashing out of the kitchen.

Molly grinned. "I don't know what you said— and so fast—but thank you, thank you, thank you."

"You're very welcome. Glad I could help."

She looked at the red bag in her hand. "Could you go for a margarita? I sure could. This has been some day. And thanks to you, it ended very happily. If you're free right now," she added, "follow me to my place. Right now, Lucy's fast asleep in the bassinet in my parents' guest room. I'll transfer her to her crib and whip us up two celebratory drinks."

He could stand here talking to her, looking at her, in her Wyoming Cowboys sweatshirt and gray yoga pants and fuzzy pink socks forever. A celebratory drink at her house? Why not. It wasn't like they'd end up in *bed*. He'd simply stay on one side of her sofa and she'd stay on the other, and they'd clink and drink and he'd leave within a half hour. "Sounds good," he said. "I could use a margarita myself. And I'm really glad everything worked out with your dad. He's a great guy."

"I could kiss you," she said, her cheeks turning red. "I mean, well, you know what I mean. It's a saying."

Oh, Molly, he thought. *I could kiss you, too.*

Chapter Eleven

Fifteen minutes later, Zeke emerged from Molly's kitchen with two margaritas, the rim of the wide-necked blue glasses dotted with salt. Just as she'd come downstairs from putting Lucy to bed, he set one down in front of her and then sat on the opposite end of the sofa.

The last time he was on this sofa, he'd kissed her. The memory was so clear. He'd tucked her curl behind her ear and then their lips met and he'd wanted more. So much more.

Molly. His everything.

"Ooh, those look festive," she said, her eyes

sparkling with anticipation. "And definitely just what the doctor ordered. Today really was *some* day."

"Was it?" he asked, thinking of what she'd had on her plate today. Nothing too hectic or out of the ordinary. But he'd been gone for a few hours, house-hunting with Danica. Perhaps during that time, she'd hit a hard patch of research in the case file he'd left her.

She sat up straight and cleared her throat. "I, um, mean with my parents. All that arguing. Oy."

"Ah. Yeah, they were really at a stalemate. I'm glad you called me."

She turned toward him. "To Dawson Solutions, Inc., saving the day again." She held up her glass.

He held up his and they clinked. "We're a good team."

She smiled and paused with her glass midway to her mouth. "I meant *you*. Once again, you helped my family in life-changing ways. Seriously, Zeke—life-changing. When we left my parents' house, I glanced in the living room window and saw my parents slow dancing."

He grinned. "Yeah, I caught that, too. They're a good team."

"Yeah, they are. And when they're both ready for a break, they'll plan a vacation and my mother will still get to see those red rocks of Utah." She took a long sip of her margarita. "Ooh, this is good." Another long sip, then another. "So tart and delicious."

He sipped his own. It *was* good. "I actually had to Google the parts. I almost put in way too much orange liqueur. But now I can add 'makes a mean margarita' to my list of skills."

They clinked again and sipped some more.

When was the last time he had a drink? A good while ago, some business function. Zeke had a beer every now and then but he rarely ever had a second. Reminded him of his dad, he supposed.

"And I appreciate what you said about my helping your family. I love the work I do. Especially when it has fast results like tonight."

"How did you do it?" she asked. "How'd you turn him around?"

Tim Orton had given Zeke blanket permission to bring in his daughter on all matters concerning the taco truck and Dawson Solutions, so he figured it was okay to tell Molly about her dad's past with the man who'd offered to buy the business.

"Wow. Why does high school have such a hold on everyone?" Molly asked. She took another sip of her margarita.

"It's when our identities are solidifying, when

we're discovering what matters to us, when our hearts are at their most vulnerable. It's no wonder people tend to remember the slights and accomplishments back then with such force." He smiled and shook his head. "And then just like that—" he snapped his fingers "—something you've been holding on to for decades disappears."

"Like your crush on my best friend."

"Exactly." He tried to picture Danica but there was just nothing. He was really and truly over a twenty-year dream—a dream based on nothing but the superficial, he realized. "Maybe I've grown up, after all." He took a sip of his drink and leaned his head back. "Maybe I should let go of everything."

Molly gave an exaggerated nod. "A fresh start. Looking at the world through who you are right now, not who you once were." She lifted her margarita and took a long sip, then another, then finished it in one full swoop.

"Definitely," he said, feeling the warmth of the tequila in his chest. He downed the rest of his margarita, too.

He couldn't take his eyes off Molly's face. And she was staring at him, her brown eyes...smoldering.

And then they both scooted closer. Closer. Then closer still.

"I like you so much, Molly."

"I like you so much, too. In fact, I—" She stopped suddenly and kissed him. Softly. She wrapped her arms around his neck, deepening the kiss. Driving him wild.

Put a stop to this, he thought. Now. "I want this, Molly. Believe me, I do. But I made a promise to both of us—"

Had that sexy beauty mark just above her right eyebrow always been there?

She lifted her face to his. Her beautiful face.

"Molly, we can't kiss again. Can. Not. I'd leave like I know I should, but I guzzled the margarita and there's no way I should drive right now. We could watch a movie and I could fall asleep in that chair."

"Oh, that chair is very uncomfortable. So let's just keep kissing and you could let that excuse go, Zeke. It's a two-person office. There's no HR department. I'm a grown woman making my own decisions. I will write out a declaration this moment that we really and truly fell for each other and therefore had to kiss. And hopefully more."

"It's not an excuse," he countered, but his voice sounded kind of light when he meant to be serious. "It's a line that shouldn't be crossed."

She held his gaze and he couldn't drag his eyes off hers. "You know, Zeke, being your admin has its advantages. Because I have a solution to our problem. A Dawson Solutions solution."

He raised an eyebrow. "And what's that?"

"Change my title so that you're not my boss."

He smiled. "It's my company. I'd still be your boss."

"Not if we had the same title. What's your title, anyway? Your business card and letterhead just says Consultant."

"*That's* my title," he said. "I like that better than president or CEO or some other highfalutin title I could have given myself. I'm a consultant. I consult."

"Well, I consult, too, really. Just in a different way than you do. I consult information all day long and work up reports. I consult my laptop to keep your client files up to date. If my title is consultant and your title is consultant, how are you my boss?"

He was dimly aware that he was giving in to this, that he was crossing a line he couldn't backtrack from. "Okay, Molly, I just changed your title. You're now a consultant at Dawson Solutions."

A slow, satisfied smile spread across her beautiful face. "Yes. And you are my sole client."

Her sexy voice lured him closer. She was so tantalizingly close, her lips just an inch away.

"So you're not my boss anymore, Zeke. That

means we can kiss all we want. And anything else."

A very low-sounding alarm went off in the back of his head but he was too taken with Molly's pink lips and the pure desire in her eyes to pay attention to it.

"You are so beautiful," he whispered, one hand winding in her lush hair while the other drew her to him. She kissed him so passionately that he allowed himself to lean back against the sofa. The loosened tie was flung off. His shirt was next.

Then hers. He sucked in a breath at the sight of her lacy black bra. Sexy, sexy, sexy.

The next thing he knew, they were in her bed in a tangle of sheets and down comforter. Naked. Exploring.

And everything Zeke had been reining in for weeks let loose.

"Oh, Zeke," Molly moaned into his ear.

And all he could think about was how very right everything about this felt right now.

The sun was rising when Molly woke up, a grin on her face like she was Sally when Meg Ryan and Billy Crystal finally slept together in *When Harry Met Sally*.

But when she glanced over at Zeke, naked next

to her in her bed, he looked just like Harry had: staring at the ceiling in a state of wide-eyed absolute shock—and regret.

Oh, foo. This was not the face of a man in love. A man who'd made love to the woman he realized he'd loved all along.

This was a man who was about to break her heart.

She sucked in a breath and let it out. "How long have you been staring at the ceiling, looking like you just made the worst mistake of your life?"

He sat up and looked at her, something close to torment in his eyes. Just what every woman wanted to see in the face of the man she loved after they had sex for the first time. "Molly, I—"

"Shouldn't have done this, can't do this, let's pretend this never happened. Do I have that right?"

He leaned his head back. "This is why I should never drink. One too-strong margarita and my inhibitions went out the window. Judgment canceled. Common sense gone." He shook his head.

"Except last night was amazing," she said, trying to keep the air of positivity she felt instead of the reality lying beside her. "Admit it."

"Yes, it was amazing. I had no doubt it would be. But it doesn't change anything, Molly."

"I'm a consultant, not your admin. Everything's fine now."

That got a brief, sad smile out of him. "Except it's not fine. I'm not…" He stopped talking and looked up at the ceiling. "You're a…"

Tears welled but then anger blinked them away. "A what? A mother? A package deal? Damned straight I am."

"And…" He looked truly pained at least. "I've been honest about where I am on that."

She frowned, not wanting to hear this. She wanted him to be past this. Because she was worth it.

He took her hand. "You need someone who can offer you forever, someone who wants to be Lucy's stepfather. I'm not that person. I never was."

She slipped her hand away. "So you said. Many times. I see otherwise in you."

"That's not really fair, though. Is it?"

Tears threatened. She couldn't take this.

He slid his legs to his side of the bed and grabbed his clothes.

Dammit. "I'm officially calling in sick, Zeke. Right now."

He turned and touched her face, then got out of bed and quickly dressed.

"I'm sorry, Molly. I am."

Don't be sorry. Be who you really are—not who you're hiding behind.

Or maybe that was wishful thinking—again—on her part all this time. He was right—he *had* told her over and over and she didn't want to believe it.

I love you, Zeke Dawson, she wanted to scream at the top of her lungs. *And I know you have serious feelings for me. Are you really just going to let me go?*

"Come back to the office when you feel ready, Molly," he said. "I need you and I don't want anything to come between our great working relationship. I'll understand if you feel otherwise, though." He let out a breath. "I messed up."

Humph, she thought. She couldn't speak.

She just flopped back against the pillows.

"I'm sorry," he said again, and then was gone.

Chapter Twelve

"Oh, Molly," Danica said. "I wish you'd told me about your feelings for Zeke all along. I could have been a support for you."

The two of them sat at the round table in Molly's kitchen, sipping the fancy hot coffee drinks Danica had brought over after Molly had called her a half hour ago, sobbing, at 7:15 in the morning. Her friend had also brought bagels with cream cheese and apricot Danish, Molly's favorite pastry.

Molly had left one big part out of what she'd shared with Danica: Zeke's longtime crush on her friend. Given that it was over now and that Danica would only feel bad for Molly's sake and quite possibly upset about the whole thing, Molly thought it was best to just keep it to herself. This was about her feelings for Zeke. And her broken heart.

"I know he has feelings for me," Molly said, biting into her Danish. "But he's so controlled by his past that he won't let himself have a future. It sucks."

Danica nodded and took a sip of her mocha latte. "It does. But I have a good feeling that Zeke will come around."

"What makes you think that?"

"Because until now, I don't think Zeke Dawson has ever been in love before," Danica said. "It's all new to him. He's probably never had his feelings for a woman pitted against that past before. Now it is."

Did Zeke love her? "So you think he just needs time? What if he chooses to be alone instead? What if he doesn't pick love?"

"He won't really have a choice. A man in love can't stay away. Being without you will be a hell of a lot worse than actually facing down his fears over marriage and parenthood."

Molly almost smiled. But she wasn't too sure about that.

"I told him I was taking a sick day," she said.

"But maybe I shouldn't. Maybe I should be right there, front and center in his office."

"I'm not a hundred percent on this, but I say take the day off. You both need a little space right now and some time to let this sit. Go in fresh tomorrow."

Molly sipped her coffee, the caffeine helping. "You're right. Thanks for coming over, Danica—especially at the crack of dawn in the freezing cold."

"Of course. Want me to bring lunch over later?"

"Nah, I'll be okay. Call me on a break, though."

"Will do." Danica bent down and wrapped her arms around Molly. "That man will be your husband someday. Mark my words."

Molly imagined herself in a wedding gown and veil, walking down the aisle to Zeke. Her heart stirred. She liked those words but she wouldn't hold her breath on that one. Still, she felt a lot better now. Thank heavens for girlfriends.

Once Danica left, Molly nibbled her pastry and finished her coffee, then took a long, hot shower. Maybe she'd drive over to Prairie City with Lucy and do a little shopping, have lunch at her parents' taco truck and distract herself from the ache in her chest.

By eleven, Molly was in Prairie City with Lucy.

At noon, they headed into the independent bookstore for their daily Story Time, which Molly only usually got to attend on weekends. She found a spot on the colorful round rug at the back of the shop, many other parents and little ones there, including a couple with their arms entwined, their toddler on Dad's lap, Mom's hand on her six-ish-months pregnant belly. Another couple sat with their baby in Dad's arms. And yet another couple had twin toddlers, one on each lap. The Story Time leader took photos, tradition for the daily activity, and Molly loved seeing her and Lucy's pictures sometimes posted on the store's blog.

Lucy on her lap, Molly smiled as the camera stopped on her. *What's different about* this *picture?* she muttered to herself. Sometimes, when she was in this type of environment, happy intact families all around her, she wanted to cry. Single odd mom out. Alone. Partnerless. And warranted or not, she'd hear in her head: *Oh, poor Lucy from a broken home...*

Lucy had a father who loved and cared about her and was there for her, plus a kind stepmother, who Molly had grudgingly stopped hating because she was wonderful with Lucy. Her baby girl had lots of family who loved her on both sides. But Molly wanted a life partner, a husband, a rock, someone who'd be equally as wonderful to her baby girl.

She'd fought so hard to get over Tim's affair and the divorce. Now she was fighting to make another man see that he loved her? That he would be a great dad?

What the hell? She deserved better than that. She'd done her work on herself like Oprah had been talking about for years. Now it was Zeke's turn.

For Zeke, the next few days were the pits. Molly had come back to work the following day, professional as always, neutral-pleasant expression, no lingering looks. She did her work, kept her head down, left for lunch at twelve thirty and returned at one fifteen. Then she'd make herself a cup of her favorite chocolate-hazelnut coffee and scroll through her phone, reading her social media accounts. Then at one thirty she'd get back to work.

She wasn't ignoring him, per se. She acknowledged him when he came in each morning. She gave him a brief smile as he passed her in and out of the office. But she *was* ignoring him. He felt the deep freeze in the office and he hated it. He missed his Molly so much that he hadn't slept more than a couple hours at a time since their night together.

And just when he couldn't take it another minute, it was Saturday and he wouldn't see her at all for two days. At least during the week she'd be sitting at her desk.

Zeke flopped over in his bed, pulling the pillow over his head like he used to as a kid when he didn't like what was going on. At least he had a busy day. At ten, he'd give his talk at the Teen Rancher's Summit and he had Dawson Solutions work to do today, as well.

He finally got out of bed and took a shower, going over his speech in his head so he wouldn't think about Molly. Then he had two mugs of strong coffee out on the back deck, the cold, crisp February air a good jolt. At 9:45 he left the cabin and headed toward the lodge, a gorgeous white clapboard building with a steep roof just a quarter mile away. The summit was being held in the second-floor event room, which overlooked Clover Mountain and land and trees as far as the eye could see. His grandparents had originally built this lodge fifty-two years ago, and his gramps used to take the six of them up here when it was too cold to play outside and let them race around on Rollerblades and skateboard to their hearts' content. A few times his gramps had found him standing by the big window, taking in the view, and Gramps would give him the history and stories about Clover Mountain. Whenever he'd visited the ranch over the past year, this view would fill him up, restore something in him. He never understood *what* exactly. He just knew the view was about peace for him. Maybe because it was connected to his grandfather, not his father.

Now, as he entered the lodge and headed past the Kid Zone, he could just make out boisterous voices of happy kids playing. He was suddenly struck by a memory, of his grandfather telling him a story about Axel's favorite goat, Flash, getting loose and running into the mountain and how their dad had taken Axel to find Flash, staying up there past midnight till the goat was brought down safely. His dad was a heavy drinker even then, and even at nine, ten years old, Zeke would understand that his grandfather's stories about Bo Dawson were to make them both wary of his father's faults and appreciative of his good points.

You'll understand your dad better when you have children of your own, he recalled his grandfather saying more than once, particularly when he was a young teenager. *Life is complicated but wonderful.*

I'm never having kids. No way, Zeke had said. His grandparents had passed when he was fifteen, and he could recall the anguish and the doubling down on the vow never to have a family of his own. Bo Dawson had been drunk at his parents' funeral, barely able to stand. His six kids had been equally furious and understanding. But that day had seeped inside Zeke's cells. He was his father's son and why create a new family only to disappoint them and hurt them because they'd love you no matter what the hell you did. That was family, wasn't it?

Zeke sucked in a breath and tried to clear his head and fill it with his talk today. Money. Business. Entrepreneurial spirit. How the future started now—if you planned for it.

When Zeke walked in, his sister-in-law Sara, the forewoman, was wrapping up her talk about general ranch management. Sara knew her stuff, and the applause she'd gotten, including wolf whistles from a group of teenage girls, made him smile. The kids were sitting at round tables with water bottles and snacks, banquet-style, and there was a table at the front of the room, meant for sitting on so the talk wouldn't feel like school or a lecture.

Noah introduced Zeke to the crowd—twenty-seven kids between thirteen and eighteen. He looked out the window perpendicular to the tables, Clover Mountain in the near distance doing its magic, restorative work on him. And then he sat down on the table, placing his Stetson beside him, and welcomed the teens, talking to them openly and honestly as Noah had suggested, mining his own memories as a teenager to relate his talk to their lives.

"As my brother said, I'm Zeke Dawson, and I moved back to Bear Ridge recently to open my own business, helping other businesses and their owners become success stories. I believe that everyone can become a success story—no matter where you start out. As you know from hearing Noah's talk, my family had it rough for a number of years. Our father was an alcoholic who drank away grocery money. I can't count the times my siblings and I, as teenagers, had to use all our strength to pull our father—dead drunk and dead weight—into the house so he wouldn't freeze to death."

He took a breath and glanced out at the mountain. "When things in your life seem too hard to surmount, when you think there's nothing more for you out there so you might as well make trouble for yourself, I'm here to tell you that there's always going to be something that flips a switch in you. Maybe it's there now. Something you love doing. Playing soccer. Drawing. Chemistry class.

Animals. You can take that thing you love and let it take you far and away. For me, that passion was business. Why does one pizza place do well and another fails? That's the question I like to answer. So when I was a junior in high school, I got a job at a pizzeria in town and studied what the owner did and why. My job was cleaning tables and mopping the floor, but I watched and learned and earned a heck of a lot more from that job than my lousy paycheck."

He looked out at the faces staring at him. No one looked bored. All the kids seemed to be listening—really listening. And it inspired him. He talked some about what he did with that paycheck, spending half and saving half, and he saw a few kids taking notes.

"When I graduated from high school," he continued, "I left town and put myself through college in Cheyenne with two jobs, one working in the mail room of a big company. Within five years, I had my own office in that company. Within ten, I was a vice president. You can be anything you want to be. Let's say you want to be an NBA player. Work for it. Who says it can happen for one kid but not you? Let's say you want to be a brain surgeon. Make it happen. Mechanic—make it happen. FBI agent—make it happen. Anything is possible."

He then launched into how to trick yourself into saving your money when you wanted to buy a new bike or video game, how to put blinders on when it came to following your heart, following your passion. You just had to keep your eye on the prize and not let anything or anyone tell you it was unattainable.

And then his talk was over, and Noah was actually hugging him. Sara had tears in her eyes and said she might have to ask him back every month. A bunch of kids came up to him to shake his hand and tell him they got a lot out of his talk. That they liked knowing it really was possible to make it on your own, that you didn't have to be a golden boy.

"Well, all that sounds good but forget it for me," a kid with dark hair and hazel eyes said as he kicked at the floor, his hood up and his shoulders bunched. He wore a My Name Is sticker on his shirt, Jeremy scrawled in blue pen. "I can like what I want and I'm never gonna be anything. My dad's in jail and my grandfather was in prison and I probably will be, too, by the time I'm nineteen."

"Your dad's in jail?" Zeke asked. "That has to be rough on you."

The kid nodded and looked at the ground.

"That stuff I was talking about—about what

you like to do, makes you feel better, gets you excited. What is that for you?"

"Forget it," Jeremy said. "It's not like it's gonna happen."

"But it could. If you *make* it happen."

The kid rolled his eyes. "I'm gonna be a social studies teacher like Mr. Reinhart? Right."

"What's he like?" Zeke asked.

"He really knows his stuff. You can tell he really cares about what happened in history. And the way he teaches it is really interesting. He talks to us with respect, too."

"That can be you in five years. You graduate, you go to college, could be community college right here in Converse County, and you get a degree in education for teaching social studies in grades seven through twelve. You get hired by a school district, and suddenly you're Mr. Reinhart, inspiring a new group of kids."

"That's how it's done? I go to college for teaching social studies?"

Zeke nodded and pulled out his card. "When you're a senior next year, you can call me and I'll help you with the process of applying to college if you want. You can utilize your school guidance counselor or any inspiring adult who'll help you. But if you need my help, you just call."

Jeremy's eyes widened. "Really? Why are you helping me?"

"Because it would have been cool if someone had done that for me when I was your age. My older brother tried, but there were five others to worry about."

The boy stared at Zeke, his expression having slowly morphed from wary to possible.

"You decide your path, Jeremy. No one else. You."

Jeremy looked back at the card. "Thank you." He nodded a few times, then put the card in his back pocket and walked away toward his table.

"I heard most of that," Noah said. "I could use you regularly with the program if you're interested. I had no idea you could be so inspiring."

Zeke laughed. "Me, either."

"I think it's the truest thing you can say to a kid—that you decide your own path. No one else. You. For a long time I let the crap I went through make my decisions."

"Yeah, I'm still doing that at age thirty-one," Zeke said, shaking his head. Who did he think he was, giving advice when he couldn't take it himself?

"So stop," Noah said. "Just decide to stop— make that your goal. When you come down to it, you're just being stubborn at your own expense. And hell, I don't even know what we're talking about—specifically, I mean."

Zeke smiled. "I'm afraid I'm gonna be like Dad. That's his blood is running in my veins and I'll screw up a kid's life. Make him feel like Jeremy."

"I'd think about what you said to Jeremy and then follow your own excellent advice."

If he wanted Molly in his life, he'd have to try.

Chapter Thirteen

On Tuesday morning, Molly stood in the doorway of Zeke's office and cleared her throat. He was reading something on his desktop, his dark hair lit up from the sunlight pouring in through the window behind him. He looked so handsome.

Her mind flashed to their night together. And how he'd left. Now it was time for *her* to leave. She wasn't going to chase a man's love. Either he did or he didn't.

All weekend she'd thought long and hard on what to do and this morning, when she'd been putting on her off-white wool pantsuit, the one she'd worn on her first day at Dawson Solutions, Inc., she'd looked at herself in the mirror and knew. Tears had welled in her eyes but she'd blinked them away.

The same thing threatened now. Good thing the light application of mascara she wore was waterproof or she'd have raccoon eyes the minute she blurted out what she'd come to say.

"Hi," he said, snapping her out of her thoughts.

She walked into his office, stopping behind the chair facing him. *Don't sit. Just say what you came to say.*

"Zeke, I love my job." *I love you.* "But this last week has just been too hard on me. I've decided to leave Dawson Solutions and I'm happy to give you two weeks' notice but I'd rather not. I'd like to finish out today by getting everything in order for my replacement and I'll even arrange for a temp and list my job opening. But I can't do this anymore."

He dropped his head in his hands, then looked up at her. "Dammit." He shook his head and said dammit a few more times.

She said nothing.

"I was afraid of this," he said.

She glared at him. "Afraid that I'd quit and you'd be out a great admin or afraid I'd walk out of your life?"

He stood up and came around his desk, leaning against it. "The latter, Molly. Of course." He shook his head again, and stood up straight, then leaned again.

At least this was rough on him. At least she had that.

She lifted her chin. She'd thought about the various ways he could react, and her plan B was dependent on it. She had to admit she was relieved that he seemed to be tied in knots. Because she sure as hell didn't want to walk out of *his* life. But she would.

"Oh," she said. "Well, in that case, you have until the end of the day to make something right between us."

A risk. One that might work in her favor. Their favor. Or one that would leave her where she'd been two minutes ago: about to quit, prepared to quit. To say goodbye to the dream that was Zeke Dawson.

He stared at her, and she could see he was thinking about it. That was a good sign.

Or again, maybe the queen of wishful thinking was at it again. She'd been her own fairy godmother but she couldn't be her own Prince Charming. She needed him to realize what he had, what *they* had, and decide that whatever had him gripped in the past needed to be cast aside.

"Five p.m.," she said, then turned and left, nervous as hell.

For most of the day, Zeke had paced his office, his head about to explode. All day, he'd felt like he'd had that little angel on one shoulder and the devil with his pitchfork on the other.

Angel: *Don't let that woman walk out of your life. She means so much to you!*

Devil: *You're just like your dad. You can't escape it. You're going to be a terrible husband, just like he was. A terrible father to that sweet baby girl. It's in your blood, your cells.*

Back and forth. Angel. Devil. Angel. Devil. Every time he thought, *Of course I'm choosing Molly over a life without her*, he'd be right back where he started.

Scared of something that made no damned sense. He wasn't his father. He wasn't anything like his father.

Yes, because you're single. Because you don't have children. Of course you're not like him. But just wait...

He'd been called a commitment-phobe since his first relationship back in high school. And with every woman since. He'd tried hard to overcome it with his last girlfriend but luckily her true colors had shown themselves before he'd twisted himself into a pretzel for her.

Molly was special. Molly was worth twisting himself into discomfort for. *Change isn't going to be easy—isn't that what you'd had to say to clients?*

At 4:59, Molly stood in his doorway again and cleared her throat. "One minute to quitting time. Either way."

No. He wasn't letting her go. There had to be a way for him to get ahead of this thing gripping him, the thing that kept him up at night and sent chills down his spine when he thought about marriage, about parenthood.

"Forty seconds," she said, eyeing her gold watch.

"Maybe we should go on a proper date," he said out of the blue. He had no idea where *that* had come from but now it seemed like a good idea. "We can take it one step at a time. You have to admit that we skipped a few steps." He turned all this over in his mind. Small steps. Yes. It didn't have to be all or nothing, a huge rush into the polar opposite of his life's plan for himself.

She tilted her head, a bit of a smile on her face.

"I'll admit that we never did go on a proper date. And I happen to be free tonight."

He smiled, relief flooding him, and reached a hand to her curl, which was springing in her face. He tucked it behind her ear. "Me, too. Pick you up at 6:45?"

"See you then."

She turned and left, the slightest scent of her perfume in the air. A proper date with Molly. That would mean dinner, perhaps slow dancing. He knew just the place to take her.

And then afterward? Who knew?

All her life, Molly had been the "plain Jane," the girl who faded into the background, even with her wild mop of curls. She'd been the woman in the beige pantsuit and sensible shoes.

Tonight, she was once again going to be her own fairy godmother and turn herself into a hot tamale—which had meant calling in the big guns: Danica Dunbar.

Now, one hour before Zeke would be picking her up, Danica looked through Molly's closet. "My goodness, how many beige pantsuits do you *own*?"

"Five, in various shades of ecru."

Danica laughed. "Well, no beige tonight, my dear." She turned and studied Molly, tilting her head to the left and to the right, clearly thinking deeply about fashion and beauty—all the things Molly never gave a thought to. "Okay, so you want to be *you*, just enhanced."

"Me, enhanced. Yes, that sounds just right."

Danica nodded and slid things on hangers, occasionally pulling something out, shaking her head, then putting it back. Repeated that four times. "Wait a minute, what do we have here?" This time she pulled out a black dress Molly had bought years ago after reading in *Wyoming Woman* magazine that every woman's closet should contain a little black dress. There had been photos of what that meant, and Molly had bought a classic sheath with a V-neck. It was more formfitting than she'd ever feel comfortable in, which was why she'd never actually worn it. "We have the dress. Now, the shoes. Please tell me you have a pair of black pumps that are not work- or walking-friendly."

"I do have black patent stilettos that my cousin Erin bought me for my bridal shower. They went with a black lace teddy my other cousin got me. Not that I ever wore that, either."

Danica stared at her like she couldn't fathom letting such treasures go to waste. She bent down and shoved shoes around. "Oh, my God," she said, emerging with the shiny pumps in her hands.

"Yes! These are perfect!" She turned and looked at Molly. "Next, outerwear other than the puffy coat and the peacoat?"

Molly thought about that. "I have a trench coat. The traditional kind."

"Hmm. I'm not feeling it for this outfit. I have at least five black wool coats. I'll drop one off after we're done here."

They might be worlds apart in many ways, but they actually wore the same size.

"Okay," her friend continued. "Outfit, check. Now jewelry. Earrings of your choice, perhaps a bangle bracelet, and you're done. Then I'll do your makeup—again, just an enhanced you. Natural but date-ish. Hair—loose. And here comes the Molly no one's ever met before."

Molly laughed. "Even me."

A half hour later, Molly gasped at herself in the mirror. She looked exactly as Danica had said: enhanced. Her dress was a little sexy, in her opinion, and she'd never choose it normally for a date, but this wasn't a normal occasion. This was her first proper date with the man she loved, the man of her dreams. The man she was going to make hers forever.

"Oh, Molly. He's going to faint. I'm going to

faint. I've never seen you look like this. Not even on your wedding day."

"I might have gone a little too poufy that day. The poufy dress and poufy hair canceled each other out."

Danica was beaming. "You look amazing. You always do, but wow."

The best part? Zeke Dawson had found her beautiful and sexy as the "Molly before." So tonight was all about showing him other tantalizing aspects of herself. If she wanted him to see *he* had other sides he had trouble accessing, then she could certainly do the same. Stepping out of the ole comfort zone—into the rest of her life.

Molly knew a sexy dress and glossy lips weren't going to make Zeke Dawson want to be her husband or Lucy's stepfather. That had to come from him.

Chapter Fourteen

Molly dabbed her favorite perfume on her wrist and behind her ears and she was ready. Any second now, Zeke would ring the doorbell and the night she'd been dreaming of since she was thirteen was finally going to happen.

Her parents were babysitting Lucy. She'd told her Mom all about falling for Zeke and how tonight was a first step toward things maybe working out between them, and Abby had insisted on watching Lucy *overnight*. Molly was not to even think about picking her up till at least noon. She'd given Molly a sly smile and a big hug before leaving with Lucy right before Molly started getting dressed for the big event.

The doorbell rang.

When she opened it, Zeke gasped.

She laughed. "I clean up well, huh?"

"You sure do. You look absolutely stunning. You always do, Molly. But tonight—whoa."

"You look amazing yourself." And he did. He wore dark pants and a charcoal button-down shirt with a jacket, his wool overcoat.

"I've made reservations for 7:15 at Arabella's in Prairie City. You once mentioned you've always wanted to go there."

Only the most romantic restaurant in Converse County. There was even a gazebo-like dance floor adjacent to the dining room.

He helped her into her snazzy black wool coat—*thank you, Danica*—and out they went. On the way to the restaurant, Zeke put music on low and they started chatting easily like old times about everything and anything—their favorite bands, TV shows, what was binge-worthy and all the restaurants they'd been to in the area. Zeke hadn't been to many in the short time he'd been back.

"Well, if we have a second date, we can go to Margarita's Mexican Café," Molly said. "The food is so good." She tilted her head. "Oh," she added.

"That's where your parents met. I'm not sure if it has good or bad associations for you."

There *would* be a second date. There had to be. And a third. And a millionth.

"It's a sweet story," he said. "Their marriage might not have lasted, but that's my history in Margarita's."

"I guess I shouldn't remind you of *our* history in margaritas," she said with a slight smile. "The drink."

"I like to be reminded of that night, Molly," he said very seriously. "I'm not proud of how I reacted the morning after, but I'll never forget that night. It was very special to me."

She was so surprised she couldn't speak for a second. "Me, too," was all she could manage.

"You know what I did this past Saturday?" he asked. "I did something that knocked some sense into me."

The Teen Rancher's Summit. He'd mentioned his brother Noah had asked him to give a talk and that he was looking forward to it. "The talk to the at-risk teenagers?" she said as though she didn't have even his non–work schedule committed to memory.

He nodded. "It went very well. And afterward, I was talking to a kid named Jeremy, sixteen years old, who couldn't seem to see beyond his everyday world, and the advice I gave him was that *he* decides his path, no one else. His future is up to him."

"That's beautiful and powerful advice." *Please apply it to yourself. Please.*

His smile was so warm that she wanted to reach out and squeeze his hand. "And between that talk with Jeremy and you about to quit my life, I got to thinking that I should mean what I say. I've got to let go of the past, how I was raised, the bad memories. I can't be controlled by what my father did or didn't do. And it's possible I've been using all that as an excuse to avoid commitment. I'm thirty-one and the longest relationship I've had is six months."

Hope soared in her chest. "So we have a real chance. Is that what you're saying?"

"That's what I'm saying." He slid his hand over to hers and she clasped it, her heart pulsating.

By the time he pulled into a parking spot at Arabella's, Molly was afraid if she pinched her arm she'd wake up in her bedroom, alone, that this was all a beautiful dream.

"Is it the dress? The lip gloss?" she quipped out of sheer nerves. Was this really happening?

He turned off the ignition and took both of her hands. "No, Molly. It's you."

She leaned forward and kissed him, pulling away just to look into his eyes. She wanted to say *I love you* but she didn't want to scare the man out into the hills. But she did love him, so much she could burst with it.

Inside the restaurant, dimly lit with oil paintings lining the pale yellow walls, they decided not to drink at all so that anything that happened between them happened because they wanted it to, not because the wine loosened their inhibitions. Molly ordered an interesting-looking pasta dish that she'd never heard of but sounded delicious, and Zeke went with the New York strip. Over dinner, they talked about their families and grandparents and places they'd been and places they wanted to go. Turned out they both wanted to visit Iceland and see the glaciers and volcanoes.

We'll go on our honeymoon, she thought giddily.

The dance floor was through an archway, and she could see a few couples slow dancing to an Ella Fitzgerald song. Once their entrees were cleared away and they both decided against dessert, he asked her to dance and led her to the cozy space, wrapping his arms around her waist. She put hers around his neck and they swayed to Frank Sinatra's "It Had to Be You."

"I can hardly believe this is really happening," she whispered. "The date, the talk in the car, this dance."

His lips moved close to her ear. "I guess this is our song."

I love you, I love you, I love you, she thought. "I'd say this proper first date is going very well."

He held her even closer. "*Very* well."

They danced to another song, and suddenly all she wanted was to be alone with him.

"My place?" she whispered.

He smiled and took her hand, leading her back to their table. As they were leaving, her phone pinged with a text.

Her mother. Uh-oh.

Honey, everything's okay but Lucy is feverish and screaming her head off. I'm sorry to ruin your date but I think she needs her mama.

Molly read the text to Zeke. "Motherhood calls." She looked at him, hard, studying his expression. Maybe this would undo tonight—the reminder that she came with a child and responsibilities that would usurp everything and anything, including and particularly a dream date.

He held her hand. "Tell you what. Why don't

we go pick up Lucy from your parents and I'll stay to help. I'm the baby whisperer of Bear Ridge, remember?"

"You sure? You can take a rain check." He was really all in, she thought, goose bumps on her arms.

"Oh, I want that rain check," he said. "But yes, I'm sure."

She texted her mother back that they'd be at their house to get Lucy in about a half hour and to give Lucy baby Tylenol.

"Well, I guess if we're going to date," she said as they headed for his car, "this is the kind of thing that'll happen. Sick baby. Sitter cancels last minute. My ex has an emergency and can't take Lucy on his scheduled weekend."

He was quiet for a moment. "This is your life. And I want to be a part of that life."

She reached a hand to his gorgeous cheek. "This date is still going very, very well."

He smiled and they drove off. Molly texted her mom to ask if Lucy was still crying, and the answer was yes. Poor baby. As much as she loved Zeke, she was itching to get to her baby and hold her, comfort her, take care of her.

As they pulled into her parents' driveway, Molly could hear Lucy crying the moment she opened the car door. The baby was wailing.

"Oh, boy. Cover your ears, Zeke."

"I'm used to it. I was at Noah and Sara's this past weekend, and both twins were shrieking their heads off. I could only get one to quiet down, though."

The door opened, and Molly's dad stood in the doorway, rocking a crying Lucy. The difference in temperature outside got Lucy's attention and she stopped crying—then saw her mother and held out her arms. Molly and Zeke hurried into the house, Molly taking Lucy and cuddling her.

"The Tylenol seems to be working," her dad said. "She's not as hot."

Molly touched her hand to Lucy's forehead. Warm but not feverish. That was a relief.

"Ah, the sound of silence," Tim said. "I can hear myself think." He turned to Zeke and extended his hand. "Nice to see you, Zeke."

Zeke shook her dad's hand. "As always."

Molly's mom came to the foyer, wrapping her cardigan sweater tight around her. "Oh, Molly, you look so lovely! Did you have a nice time?"

"It was wonderful and thank you. I got the text just as we were leaving so it was good timing."

Abby Orton smiled. "Oh, glad to hear. I held out for as long as I could but I could see she wouldn't calm down until she was in your arms." She turned to Zeke. "Is Arabella's as romantic as I've heard?

I'm thinking that we'll go for our thirty-fourth anniversary."

"It is," Zeke said. "They have a dance floor in a beautiful little gazebo-like area next to the dining room."

Lucy started to fuss, so Molly shifted the baby in her arms. "Well, we'll get going."

"I'll follow you home," Tim said. "In case you need backup."

"That's my job tonight," Zeke said. "Moral support, making coffee, slicing pie."

Molly saw the look that passed between her parents. A very *pleased* look.

"That's very kind of you, Zeke," her mom said. "Well, honey, call us if you need us. But looks like you've got everything covered."

Zeke borrowed a car seat from Molly's dad, and in a few minutes they were at Molly's house, Lucy fast asleep.

"I'll transfer her to the crib," Molly said once they were inside. "Why don't you see what looks good for dessert in the fridge. Want to pick a movie or TV show? Something not too engrossing just in case Lucy wakes up."

"I'm on it," he said.

She took Lucy to the nursery, her sleeping daughter's forehead feeling back to normal.

And Zeke Dawson was on her sofa. Waiting for her.

The night might have had a little detour, but he was still here.

"I'm scared to jinx myself," she whispered to Lucy as she set her precious girl in her crib and gently caressed her cheek. "But I think we're over the hump with Zeke."

Anticipation swirling, she headed back downstairs.

She was in Zeke's arms within two minutes, the pie and the TV forgotten.

A cry woke Zeke and he glanced at the alarm clock on Molly's side of the bed: 2:14 a.m. Molly stirred and turned, fast asleep, her beautiful brown curls everywhere. He gently caressed her hair and got out of bed, pulling on his pants, then headed to the nursery. Another cry sounded.

"On my way, Lucy," he whispered.

She stood in her crib, holding on to the railing and then lifting her arms.

And he froze. Just for a second, but a hesitation gripped him.

She stared up at him with her big brown eyes, so like her mother's. He picked her up and she immediately grabbed his ear, but instead of it making him laugh like it usually did, he felt a strange zap in his chest as a cold sweat broke out on the back of his neck.

What was going on with him? This was Lucy. Adorable, sweet Lucy. And he was the baby whisperer of Bear Ridge.

This is what life will be like, he thought. *I'll be responsible for this baby—not like a doting, visiting uncle, but as a father figure. Everything I do will matter in her life, affect her.*

The cold sweat on his neck turned into pinpricks. Why was he reacting like this? He'd gone through this—he knew who he was. Of course he'd be a good father figure to Lucy.

But will you? How do you know? Your work will get in the way and take your time and energy and you won't rush into the nursery to see why Lucy is crying. You'll ignore her, hope she soothes herself back to sleep. Or you'll just let Molly deal.

And then you and Molly will argue.

You used to help and now you don't, she'd say, her beautiful face angry. *You've changed.*

Have I? Or was I always this way, he'd counter.

He sat down on the rocking chair, Lucy against his chest, but instead of cherishing the sweet weight of her, the baby-shampoo scent of her, he just felt... wrong. Wrong, wrong, wrong.

He thought he could do this, that he could overcome his past, blaze his own path, but he'd always known he was really meant to be on his own, a lone wolf.

He stared out the window at the evergreens and bare trees in the moonlight. When it seemed safe to put Lucy back in her crib without her waking, he did.

And then he went back to Molly's bedroom. She looked so beautiful, lying there sleeping.

You're going to disappoint her eventually.

You're Bo Dawson's son.

He tried to lay back down but he couldn't bring himself to do so. He wrote a note.

Molly, I'm very sorry. But I need to go. —Z

He got dressed and tiptoed out of the room. He was halfway toward the door when a light turned on behind him. He turned around to find Molly in a bathrobe, holding the note, so many emotions on her face that he couldn't pick out just one.

She shook her head. "For a solutions guy, you sure are focused on only the problem."

"Maybe there is no solution here. Maybe I'm just really not meant to be a husband and father. I made that decision a long time ago and maybe it's just too ingrained. I wanted to give this a try, Molly. But I guess—"

"Or maybe you could decide that you love me and Lucy and let *that* call the shots instead," she interrupted. "If you do love us."

He looked at her, wishing the right words would come, but the cold sweat had moved into his stomach and into his throat.

She waited.

He said nothing.

"Just go," she said, and turned and ran away.

I wish I could be different, he wanted to call after her.

But he left and then sat in his car until the cold turned his hands numb.

Chapter Fifteen

On Wednesday morning, Zeke arrived at the office to find a temp from the employment agency waiting outside. Apparently, Molly had made the arrangements yesterday and had left detailed instructions since he'd only made her cutoff by a minute. The temp was experienced and pleasant, but every time Zeke walked toward the reception area, he felt both a sense of shock—who was this strange person?—and sadness. *You brought this on yourself, genius*, he reminded himself.

On Thursday, he went through the motions at work, grateful he could do some of his job on autopilot. The sight of someone else at Molly's desk kept doing him in, though, making mincemeat of his concentration. He took long walks down Main Street and then drove around to relook at the houses Danica had shown him, trying to imagine himself in one of them with a family. But that icy shield seemed to wrap around him again and he drove back to Dawson Solutions, forcing himself to focus.

On Friday Zeke stared out the window of his office, stared out the window of his bedroom, stared up at the ceiling. Had he ever felt like this before? Like he was being torn apart? Not like this. He saw Molly's face, Lucy's brown eyes, constantly. Thought of them constantly. And this certainty that he wasn't cut out for marriage and fatherhood— it was better than this torment that he was going through? He felt like hell. How could this be better?

Saturday at noon was Ford's housewarming party, so Zeke headed into town to find something Ford might like for the new place and to buy presents for his nieces and nephews, who'd all be there. For a split second he almost called Molly to ask what he should get Ford. Candlesticks? A hearth set for the fireplace? He wandered around Main Street, going in and out of stores until he saw it—the perfect gift for Ford. A good-size abstract watercolor painting of a man in a rowboat out to sea. Then he realized that was actually himself; *Zeke* was the one out to sea. He put that painting back and chose the watercolor of a man walking in the woods. He headed to the toy store next and got each little relative something small but special, wrapped in bright paper. But when he passed the teething toys and board books, especially the ones with chewable edges for teething babies like Lucy, his heart sagged and dropped.

He missed Molly. He missed Lucy.

He still didn't understand what had happened at her house, why he'd reacted the way he had. On one hand, he did understand—the reality that *that* would be his future had grabbed hold and he couldn't shake the echo in his head: *not cut out for fatherhood. You'll fail. You'll disappoint them. You'll hurt them.*

He sat in his car in the parking lot, thinking, thinking, thinking, and then it was time to head to the party.

As he glanced around the living room, looking for Ford, he did a double take. Danica Dunbar was standing beside the buffet table, chatting away with Ford, and unless he was seeing things, there was something going on between the two.

He'd told his brother that his crush on Danica was over, that he'd very unexpectedly fallen for someone else.

He figured Danica knew all about what a heel Zeke was; she was Molly's best friend and she must know what had happened. But as he approached them, Danica smiled warmly and said it was nice to see him again.

Zeke managed a smile. "Nice to see you, too."

"I mentioned to you that Danica is the one who showed me this house," Ford said. "Can't have a housewarming without the Realtor who found you the perfect home." His brother glanced at Danica, and yesiree, he could tell Ford was interested. Of course, Zeke didn't know Danica very well, but she sure seemed unable to drag her eyes off his brother.

With two hands he gave Ford the cumbersome painting, which the store owner had nicely wrapped in silver paper with a big red bow. "Happy housewarming," Zeke said. "This is for you."

"Is it a vase?" Ford joked, taking the painting and leaning it against the wall of a console table so he could rip off the wrapping paper. "Wow, I love this painting. In fact, I think it would look great right above this table. Thanks."

Ford's attention was back to something Danica

said, about the blues and greens in the painting. He wondered if Molly knew that Danica was here, surrounded by Dawsons.

Molly had once said she couldn't see Zeke and Danica together. Now, of course, that made sense. They'd never been a match. But Ford and Danica— he could definitely see it, and that was despite what his brother had said the day Zeke had come to see the farmhouse for the first time: *I said black, she said white. I said up, she said down.* Given the way they were looking at each other, the adversarial thing was working for them. Chemistry was funny that way; you just never knew.

Except for the part where Danica had told Zeke that she wasn't sure if she wanted kids. And Ford definitely did—six, in fact. But like Zeke had always said, the right person could turn you around.

He froze again. *The right person, the right person...*

Someone tapped him on the shoulder, and he ended up chatting with an old neighbor, then he found his siblings one by one and handed out the toys he'd brought.

"One of the best uncles in the world," his sister said with a grin as she watched him hand her baby son, Tony, his gift, an orange-and-yellow stuffed dog with floppy ears.

She held out Tony, clutching his new stuffy, and Zeke took his nephew, cuddling him to his chest. This didn't feel remotely scary. Uncle: safe. Father: terrifying.

"How did you, Noah, Axel and Rex do it?" Zeke whispered. "Go from feeling just like I do to being great parents? Why can't I? What the hell is wrong with me, Daisy?"

His sister patted the big easy chair by the window, and Zeke sat, giving Tony a little bounce. She sat in the chair beside his. "Are we talking about Molly?"

He nodded. "I took a step forward, thinking I could do this, that I could look forward to a future with her and her baby daughter. But then the other night, I froze. I was taking care of Lucy in her nursery, just holding her like this because she'd woken up in the middle of the night, and I just felt *wrong*. I couldn't get out of there fast enough. How could I feel like that when I love—"

Zeke froze again.

...her.

He loved Molly. He loved her with all his heart. And he loved her baby girl.

"Well, there you go," Daisy said with a gentle smile. "That's why you're scared out of your mind. You love Molly and you love Lucy and you're afraid you're going to be like Dad. Just like we all were. Until love won out."

"How does love win out? I mean, how do you make the fear of being a bad parent, a bad spouse, go away just like that?"

"Love wins because you can't imagine living without them. Because they're a part of you. They become more important than anything else. And no offense, Zeke, but given how crappy you look with your mussed hair and dark circles under your eyes, you're clearly miserable without them. Unable to think, sleep, eat. Isn't that nuts? All you have to do is be happy and yet you're standing in your way. Breaking the heart of the woman you profess to love. Breaking your own heart."

Breaking Molly's heart… He couldn't bear that.

"God, Zeke, if you can't do it for yourself, do it for Molly. Let the past go. All of it. It's just a tiny piece of who you are."

You decide your own path… He kept hearing it, echoing in his head.

"Call her right now," Daisy said. "Go see her. The way you feel when you look at her, Zeke— *that* should call the shots."

He missed Molly so much. He needed her. He loved her.

Love. All this time, that was what he'd been so afraid of. Not marriage and not parenthood. Love.

He pulled out his phone and texted.

Can we talk? Please?

His held his breath. He deserved all her anger, all her hurt, all her disappointment. He had no idea how she'd react.

His phone pinged a second later.

I'm at the taco truck in PC. It's a family affair today.

Family affair.

"Go," Daisy said. "Your future awaits."

At her tiny station in the food truck, Molly diced the last tomato for the chunky salsa, wondering what Zeke would say. He'd apologize, she figured. For how he acted. For leaving. Her. Them—her and Lucy. He'd probably ask her to come back to the office. Danica had texted her about an hour ago to mention that Zeke had arrived at Ford's housewarming party and looked like absolute hell, which had made Molly feel better and then worse. She didn't want Zeke to be miserable.

I'm sticking to my dating hiatus, Danica had added, but wow is Ford hot.

That had made Molly smile. She'd give the dating hiatus another day at most. Maybe even by the end of the housewarming party. Dawsons were simply that irresistible. And nice—even if some of them, *one* of them, was beyond stubborn.

Molly finished the tomato, trying to keep her mind on her task so she wouldn't cut her finger off. She was now helping out on weekends during the lunch rush, chopping, slicing, replenishing the napkin dispenser. It was past two o'clock and the line had quieted down. Molly's mom was sitting up front in the passenger seat with Lucy, who'd just had her own lunch while Nana read her a story.

"Isn't that Zeke's car?" her dad said, gesturing out the order window.

Molly came over and looked out. "Yup. He wants to talk." Her eyes welled, and she tried to blink back the tears.

"A guy that smart isn't going to let the best thing that ever happened to him go, Molly."

"Oh, Dad," she said, throwing her arms around him.

She went up front, put on her peacoat and hopped out. Zeke looked as bad as he could look, which meant still gorgeous but very tired.

"You might not want to stand too close," she said to him. "I probably smell like tomatoes and onions. I've been chopping for salsa."

"Oh, I want to get *very* close. I love everything about you, Molly Orton. Your hair, your face, your body, your brain and the fact that yes, you do smell like salsa right now. I love you. I'm sorry it took me so long to realize what I have."

Molly stood stock-still. "You love me?"

"I love you and Lucy more than anything. I built up some strong defenses against what scared me most. I thought that was fatherhood. But what I was really scared of was *love*. In general. And specifically. But I do love you. If you'll forgive me, if you'll give me a second chance, I'll spend my life proving to you how much."

She threw her arms around him and kissed him.

"I'm so sorry I hurt you—twice," he said, wrapping her in a hug. "I'll be making that up to you and then some."

"Yeah, you will," she said with a grin. "And at least it was all part of getting us to this moment. I love you, too, Zeke. So much."

Molly's mother came out of the truck, holding Lucy. "Your dad needs me on lettuce shredding, so would one of you mind taking the baby?"

"Ba ga!" Lucy said, holding out her arms to

Zeke. She wore thick fleece pj's with a bear ears hoodie.

"I wouldn't mind at all," Zeke said, holding out his arms. Of course, the moment he had her snuggled against him, Lucy reached her little fingers to his ear and grabbed on with a giggle. "Hey, Lucy, if your mother agrees to marry me, I'm going to be your stepdaddy. I promise you right now, I'll love you and care for you with all my heart."

Molly gasped, her eyes welling.

"My precious girl," Zeke continued, his eyes so tender on Lucy. "Whenever those arms of yours reach out to me, I'll be there. I'll never let you down, I'll never neglect you, I'll never disappoint you. I love you and I'll be the best stepfather there ever was. Know why? Because I said so. If only I'd known a lot earlier it was that simple. That I decide my own path."

"Oh, Zeke," Molly whispered, dabbing away tears.

Molly caught her mom's eyes widening, Abby's hand flying to her heart.

"Oh, my goodness," Abby said. "Am I actually interrupting a proposal?" She hurried inside, and Molly glanced at the order window to see her parents staring out, moony expressions on both their faces.

Zeke touched Molly's cheek and the errant spiral curl that had escaped her ponytail. "So I was thinking we could be partners in life, partners in business, partners in parenthood. If you're interested."

Molly actually swooned. She might faint with happiness. "Oh, I'm interested."

"Maybe you could take Lucy for a minute? I need my hands for this."

She took her daughter, holding her close, barely able to breathe, to think.

Zeke got down on one knee and held out a black velvet box. He opened it, a gorgeous diamond ring sparkling in the February sunlight. "Will you marry me, Molly?"

She was speechless for a moment. "You think I'd say no to making my own twenty-year-old dream come true?"

He slightly tilted his head. "Wait, *your* twenty-year-old dream?"

"I've been secretly in love with you since seventh grade, Zeke Dawson. So yes, I will absolutely marry you."

"Ah," he said with a smile. "Suddenly a few things make more sense. Yup, Molly Orton, I'll be making up a few things to you. Count on it." As he stood, his gorgeous blue eyes sparkled like the diamond ring, which he slid on her finger. He kissed her, then kissed Lucy on the cheek. "Like I always said, I knew the right woman could turn me around."

"I kind of love how *neither* of us knew I was the right woman. Well, I did after a while. But I waited twenty years, what was another couple weeks?" She kissed him, her heart so full.

And for someone who'd never believed in fairy tales, Molly's longtime crush on Zeke had a very happy ending.

* * * * *

Don't miss Melissa Senate's next book in the Dawson Family Ranch Series,
Wyoming Matchmaker,
available April 2021!

#2821 HIS SECRET STARLIGHT BABY
Welcome to Starlight • by Michelle Major

Former professional football player Jordan Shaeffer's game plan was simple: retire from football and set up a quiet life in Starlight. Then Cory Hall arrives with their infant and finds herself agreeing to be his fake fiancée until they work out a coparenting plan. Jordan may have rewritten the dating playbook...but will it be enough to bring this team together?

#2822 AN UNEXPECTED FATHER
The Fortunes of Texas: The Hotel Fortune • by Marie Ferrarella

Reformed playboy Brady Fortune has suddenly become guardian to his late best friend's little boys, and he's in *way* over his head! Then Harper Radcliffe comes to the rescue. The new nanny makes everything better, but now Brady is head over heels! Can Harper move beyond her past—and help Brady build a real family?

#2823 HIS FOREVER TEXAS ROSE
Men of the West • by Stella Bagwell

Trey Lasseter's instant attraction to the animal clinic's new receptionist spells trouble. But Nicole Nelson isn't giving up on her fresh start in this Arizona small town—or the hunky veterinary assistant. They could share so much more than a mutual affection for animals—and one dog in particular—if only Trey was ready to commit to the woman he's already fallen for!

#2824 MAKING ROOM FOR THE RANCHER
Twin Kings Ranch • by Christy Jeffries

To Dahlia King, Connor Remington is just another wannabe cowboy who'll go back to the city by midwinter. But underneath that city-slicker shine is a dedicated horseman who's already won the heart of Dahlia's animal-loving little daughter. But when her ex returns, Connor must decide to step up with this family...or step out.

#2825 SHE DREAMED OF A COWBOY
The Brands of Montana • by Joanna Sims

Cancer survivor Skyler Sinclair might live in New York City, but she's always dreamed of life on a Montana ranch. And at least part of that fantasy was inspired by her teenage crush on reality TV cowboy Hunter Brand. The more he gets to know the spirited Skyler, the more he realizes that he needs her more than she could ever need him...

#2826 THEIR NIGHT TO REMEMBER
Rancho Esperanza • by Judy Duarte

Thanks to one unforgettable night with a stranger, Alana Perez's dreams of motherhood are coming true! But when Clay Hastings literally stumbles onto her ranch with amnesia, he remembers nothing of the alluring cowgirl. Under her care, though, Clay begins to remember who he is...and the real reason he went searching for Alana...

HSECNM0221

"We need to get our story straight," she reminded him.

His smile faded. "It's best not to offer too many details.
We met in Atlanta, and now we have Ben."

She turned to face him, adjusting the lap belt as she
shifted. "Your family's not going to question you showing
up with a six-month-old baby? Like maybe you would
have mentioned it to them prior to now?"

One bulky shoulder lifted and lowered. "I told you we
aren't close."

"Your mom not knowing she has a grandchild is a bit
more than 'not close,'" Cory felt compelled to point out.
"Will she be upset we aren't married?"

"I'm not sure."

Her stomach tightened at his response. "Will she want to have a relationship with Ben after this weekend?"

"Good question."

"I have a million of them where that came from," she said. "I don't even know how your father died."

"Heart attack."

"Sudden." She worried her lower lip between her teeth. There were so many potential potholes for her to tumble into this weekend, and based on the tight set of his jaw, Jordan was in no shape to help navigate her through it. In fact, she had the feeling she'd be the one supporting him and he'd need solace well beyond a distraction.

"Can you answer a question with more than two words?" She was careful to make her voice light and was rewarded when his posture gentled somewhat.

"I suppose so."

"A bonus word. Nice. I'm sorry about your father's death," she said, giving in to the urge to reach out and place her hand on his arm.

Don't miss
His Secret Starlight Baby *by Michelle Major,*
available March 2021 wherever
Harlequin Special Edition books and ebooks are sold.

Harlequin.com

Don't miss the third book in the heartfelt and irresistibly romantic Forever Yours series by

CARA BASTONE

"An utterly satisfying and delicious read. One for the keeper shelf!" —Jill Shalvis, *New York Times* bestselling author, on *Just a Heartbeat Away*

Order your copy today!

HQNBooks.com

PHCBBPA0321

Mary Trace was one of those freaks of nature who actually loved first dates. She knew she was an anomaly, should maybe even be studied by scientists, but she couldn't help herself. She loved the mystery, the anticipation. She always did her blond hair in big, loose curls and—no matter what she wore—imagined herself as Eva Marie Saint in *North by Northwest*, mysterious, inexplicably dripping in jewels and along for whatever adventure the night had in store. Besides, it had been a while since she'd actually been on a first date, so this one was especially exciting.

"I was expecting someone…younger."

Reality snuffed out Mary's candle. The surly-faced blind date sitting across from her in this perfectly lovely restaurant had just called her *old*. About four seconds after she'd sat down.

Sure, this apparent *prince* wasn't exactly her type either, with his dark hair neatly parted on one side, the perfect knot in his midnight blue tie, the judgmental look in his eye. But she'd planned to at least be polite to him. She'd had some great dates with men who weren't her physical ideal. She certainly didn't point out their flaws to them literally the second after saying hello.

"Younger," Mary repeated, blinking.

The man blinked back. "Right. You must be, what, in your late thirties?"

Mary watched as his frown intensified, his shockingly blue eyes narrowing in their appraisal of her, a cruel sort of humor tipping his mouth down.

A nice boy, Estrella had said when she'd arranged the date. *You'll see, Mary. John is a rare find in a city like this. He's got a good job. He's handsome. He's sweet. He just needs to find the right girl.*

Well, Mary faced facts. All mothers thought their sons were nice boys. And just because Estrella Modesto happened to be the kindest mammal on God's green earth didn't mean she didn't have one sour-faced elitist for a son.

"Thirty-seven," Mary replied, unashamed and unwilling to cower under the blazing critique of his bright blue eyes. "My birthday was last week."

"Oh." His face had yet to change. "Happy birthday."

She'd never heard the phrase said with less enthusiasm. He could very well have said, *Happy Tax Day*.

"Evening," a smooth voice said at Mary's elbow. Mary looked up to see a fairly stunning brunette smiling demurely down at them. The waitress was utter perfection in her black vest and white button-down shirt, not a hair out of place in her neat ponytail. Mary clocked her at somewhere around twenty-two, probably fresh out of undergrad, an aspiring actress hacking through her first few months in the Big Apple.

"Evening!" Mary replied automatically, her natural grin feeling almost obscene next to this girl's prim professionalism.

Mary turned in time to catch the tail end of John's appraisal of the waitress. His eyes, cold and rude, traveled the length of the waitress's body.

Nice boy, Estrella had said.

Mary knew, even now, that she'd never have the heart to tell Estrella that nice boys didn't call their dates old and then mentally undress the waitress. Mary was a tolerant person, perhaps too tolerant, but there were only so many feathers one could stuff into a down pillow before it snowed poultry.

"Right," Mary said, mostly to herself, as John and the waitress both looked at her to order her drink. How *nice* of him to pull his eyes from the beautiful baby here to serve him dinner. She turned to the waitress. "I think we need a minute."

Mary took a deep breath. She asked herself the same question she'd been asking herself since she'd been old enough to ask it—which, according to John Modesto-Whitford, was probably about a decade and a half too long. *Can I continue on?* If the answer was yes, if she conceivably could continue on through a situation, no matter how horrible, she always, always did.

Don't miss
Flirting with Forever *by Cara Bastone,*
available January 2021 wherever HQN books
and ebooks are sold.

HQNBooks.com